WAITING

IMPATIENTLY

ANDREW H. HOUSLEY

WAITING

IMPATIENTLY

atmosphere press

To my Sujata for your faith and healing.
R.P. for your courage and compassion.

AUTHOR'S NOTE

This is a story of self-transformation found through the painful catalyst of sorrow. The struggle here is real, the texture gritty, the characters at times despicable, but all the while with any luck, relatable. Transformation does not arrive fully formed and instantly baked into the cake in this tale. The protagonist's thoughts, actions, and words share the natural human condition of soul-searching in an inhospitable emotional landscape. Some readers may find parts of this story hard to read due to offensive language or adult situations. So, to those readers, I say that self-awareness, personal transformation, and the struggles of life itself are sometimes revolting, vulgar, and inconveniently repugnant. My wish is that you find your way unhurried through these awkward moments to witness the genuinely delicate loveliness that is metamorphosis.

-A.H.H.

"How did the snake get out of its skin?"
-    Television, "Friction"

CHAPTER 1

Through the thin walls, I can hear their meaningless conversation. I'd heard all the lame attempts of verbal foreplay bathed in cheap alcohol a hundred times before. Why all the pretense? She's a prostitute—stated as a fact, not a judgment. Even without seeing her face, I know that her laugh is fake. It makes me sad. Sad in knowing that she not only had to endure this fat man's boring stories told with his almost laughable southern drawl, to be followed by the most unerotic of sexual acts ever performed. Sweaty ugly fat men smothering beautiful women—a story older than time itself.

"My Papa used to say..." starts every sentence. What man at 58 uses the term "Papa" to describe his father? "...there's more than one way to skin a cat," he continues.

"Who's skinning a cat, and for what reason?" I think

to myself.

"Really, oh my Gawd, that's like sooo interesting, like really? I never like thought about it like that," her rehearsed reply followed by an insincere giggle.

I sense that this profession was new to her. She was trying too hard. Her awkwardness creates silence. Ice cubes bang inside a rocks glass, breaking the lull, but only briefly. Followed by more embarrassing silence.

"Just get to it already!" I think. "If not for her sake, then mine!"

"This is a nice place." The sound of her high heels clumsily clicking across the hardwood floors annoys me. I imagine that she was touching things with her fingertips in an attempt to appear sexy, but with every word she speaks, the sex appeal falls away and fails, revealing a bland, childlike uneasiness.

"You have such a nice place here with all the furniture and stuff."

"My papa said this is just a place where I laid my head."

"Your papa sounds like a really smart guy," she toys with him. "Is this like the little girl's room?"

"Well, it's for boys AND girls."

"I just need like a minute of privacy to touch up my lipgloss. You know and some other like girl stuff. Is that ok?"

"My papa used to say, 'Don't do a rain dance if you don't see no clouds.'"

"Hehe."

I hear the bathroom door close, followed by a gulping and then an empty glass full of ice cubes as it touches the marble countertop—a little liquid courage for the fat man. The toilet flushes, and the bathroom door opens.

"Well, are you ready?" she offers.

"FINALLY!" I mutter to myself.

"My papa always used to say, 'Nothing falls into the mouth of a sleeping fox.'"

If I believed in Jesus, I would have asked him for some strength to keep me from laughing out loud.

They make their way into his bedroom, the barn door sliding shut. I try not to imagine what is going on in there. I try to think about something, anything else. Was the moon landing faked? Why does asparagus make my pee stink? When you meet your master, what will you do? Enough with the silly Buddhist koans already. I don't have time for that nonsense and these seemingly absurd riddles right now. I need something. Anything! I refuse to let anything going on in that room to attach itself to me in any form.

"Push-ups! I'll do lots of push-ups to keep my mind occupied." I jump out of bed and onto the floor. "1, 2, 3, 4, 5, 6, 7, 8."

The barn door slides open.

"Thanks, Mike, that was like fun." The front door opens and closes. She got what she came for and left. Are you kidding me?! All the foreplay, inane chatter, alcohol, and the actual deed itself took less than three minutes? It hardly seemed worth all the trouble.

This level of introspection makes my head ache. Why must I pour myself over every micro detail with unnecessarily painstaking scrutiny? Countless fictitious scenarios are jostling around on the battleground of my fertile imagination. My bitter, brittle heart is so full of contempt and anger.

"You shouldn't be thinking like this!" I chastise myself.

"You know better! Why do you continue to do this to yourself?" My constant internal dialogue rages.

As I climb into bed, I think about how little Man had evolved from his most basic and primal beginnings. As sleep arrives, I think of sweaty ugly fat men smothering beautiful women for less than three minutes at a time. The pushups and koans failed me—let the nightmares come.

The morning arrives earlier than normal. Sleep had become a personal and inconsistent hellscape. A few hours of dreamless slumber, throat-punched with endless tossing. Eyes now open, not wanting to wallow in the shallow pool of regrettable memories that usually arrive with the sunrise, I tear myself from the sheets. Bathroom. Coffee. Water and a fresh stick of incense lit for my morning offering. A pitiful offering, truth be told, but an offering nonetheless. Onto my knees. Hands to heart. I attempt to hold back a yawn not to insult or devalue the meaning of thankfulness I wish to convene to the serene Buddha in front of me.

The Buddha before me was carved from a single piece of hardwood standing almost ten inches high. In the female form, she is the definition of grace, tranquility, and calm. The length of her robes so exquisitely and delicately carved that it appeared she sat in the eye of a wild windstorm. You can sense the chaos that surrounds all while her expression remains unchanged. Is she smiling or laughing at me? Some days, it's hard to tell. I like to believe she knows what's going on, but she may be just as rudderless and confused in this world as I am. What a pair we make.

She was a gift in every sense of the word. Given to me years prior by my ex-mother-in-law after one of her many lavish vacations to central China. The carving is probably illegal to be outside of the country since my guess is to say she is over 150 years old. I invited her into my life because a Buddha chooses you and not the other way around. She accepted, undoubtedly knowing the mayhem that consumed my life. Instantly, a constant companion. She weathered countless moves, always finding a place of distinction in each of my homes.

My "home" was nothing more than a small dark room crammed into a dollhouse-sized bottom-floor apartment that I desperately rented from my friend and friend to prostitutes, Mike. Desperate, not from a lack of funds but from a lack of time. I did my best to provide her the place of honor that she deserved. A simple small, raised alter surrounded by plants on a shallow windowsill. But just as equally pathetic as today's offering, so too is her current address—the lowest of the lows for me.

The building sits on a steep hill in deep woods. Looking down through the leafless trees of winter, you can see a golf course fairway. On more than one occasion, I heard the loud 'whack' of a metal club striking a golf ball. A piercing howl of "Fuuuuccckk! Forrrreee!!" moaned from below. Ricocheting through the trees, the ball had lost its desired course. Now deep among the brittle leaves, hidden from sight with no master left to serve. Its immediate purpose now complete. The patient wait to return to the Earth began.

"How long will that take?"

"At least a hundred years."

CHAPTER 2

With the morning 'thank yous' complete, I turn on my phone. Insert my earbuds. Begin my search for today's musical distraction. Music is the soundtrack to my memories; its constant cues texture and frame my personal and emotional landscape. Attempting to find a song that retains no echo to the past is an almost insurmountable task. The search begins again. Iggy Pop? I've nothing but respect for you, Mr. Osterberg, but lust for life is a pill a bit too hard for me to swallow today. Richard Hawley? No love songs, please. The Smiths? Can't you see that I'm barely hanging on here? Roxy Music? I said no, LOVE SONGS! Other nameless artists are briefly considered and dismissed. Stopping to press play on Suede's 'By The Sea,' I always loved the bass line—required and effortless. Brett Andersen's high-pitched nasally whine enters, and I am pulled back 25 years into the past.

He can walk out anytime
Anytime he wants to walkout
That's fine
He can walk out anytime
Across the sand, into the sea
Into the brine
And when I start my new life
I won't touch the ground
I'm gonna try hard this time
Not to touch the ground

Memories of my college friend Nathan form. A rabid Suede fan. So much so, he named his golden retriever Suede. Not overly creative, but I admired his dedication. For me, his commitment was not to the band or music but more to Brett Andersen's androgyny. His sexuality was mercurial and slippery when you tried to put a finger on it. It did not surprise me that Nathan, having recently told the world that he was gay, found himself attracted to Brett's 'best of both worlds' sex appeal.

"They are the best band ever!"

A bold statement.

"The best? A bit melodramatic, don't you think?" I poked the nerve.

"Fuck you."

Disarmed, I had no reply. Nothing trumps a heartfelt full-throated 'fuck you.'

For the next two decades and through numerous hit-or-miss tunes, Nathan maintained his obedient dedication to Brett. His larger, more determined dedication to alcohol was his final undoing. His return to the Earth began eight years ago.

"I'm a gay man that was never loved or even had sex with another man. Who could ever love me?"

The thought of him dying alone with this tattooed on his heart makes my own heart ache. Everyone, even Nathan, deserved love, even for just a few tiny milliseconds. His immediate purpose was never really complete. Just crudely truncated.

"How long did it take?"

"Almost 41 years."

He can walk out anytime

Anytime he wants to walk out

That's fine

The song ends, and I'm back. In the kitchen now. Breakfast. Oatmeal, yogurt, blueberries, peanut butter, and chia. The barn door opens. Mike appears holding a pile of dirty bedsheets. Presumably, the same set of sheets involved in last night's record-setting three-minute intense session of passionate love-making. We can't all be gold medal winners.

"Good morning."

"Morning. I hope I didn't disturb you last night," he says as he stuffs the sheets in the washing machine. Followed with a copious amount of detergent and bleach. Water set to HOT. Some regrets can't be washed away, even in the hottest of water.

"Nope, you didn't disturb me. I didn't even hear you." I lie. Changing the subject, "Do you think they are going to lock us down?"

"Nah, it's just a scare tactic by the government. They can't shut down the world! Where would I eat?"

I hadn't rented a room from him for long, but I knew Mike didn't know how to cook. I had never seen him eat a home-cooked meal or eat at home, not even a bowl of cereal. Every meal is consumed in a restaurant. I could never decide if this was pure overindulgence or pathetic laziness. I'm leaning towards the latter.

"I don't know about that. It seems pretty real to me. A lot more than a scare tactic."

"Like my papa used to say, 'Let's pretend like I'm from Missouri and show me.' Until then, for the lack of a better word, I think it's bullshit—excuse my language," Mike drawls.

I laugh at the stupidity of the comment, not the joke. He didn't recognize the difference.

"All I'm saying is that you should be careful. Not to worry you, but this could get ugly fast." I hoped that he would take it as a hint to stop bringing the prostitutes home.

"Worry? You know me, I never worry. I'm always the first guy in the pool after eating lunch."

Hint not received, but I'm sure his papa would undoubtedly be proud of his willful ignorance. We say our goodbyes as he heads out the front door. Before the door locks shut, he flings a "Be safe."

Was that meant for him or me? And I am alone again. If being alone is an art form, then I'm presently the Rembrandt of the medium. My current canvas is a comically small apartment with low spackled ceilings, dark hardwood plank floors, and minuscule windows. The dense thicket of trees outside makes the sun's attempts to illuminate the place nearly impossible. Rooms full of cheap furniture—oversized and overstuffed. Navigating the space is unfeasible without banging a knee or bruising a rib. A cave furnished by Rooms To Go.

"You know what would tie this whole place together?"

Cocked heads lean in with curious interest.

"Some primitive hand-painted ox blood cave art!"

"I'm sorry to inform you, sir, but we are currently out of stock."

And in that instant, my hopes of being a celebrity interior designer are dashed.

Begrudgingly, I must return to my real-life profession as a yoga teacher. And with that, let the torrent of insults, stereotypes, and clichés about male yoga teachers rain down on me.

"Are you gay?"

"No."

"All those sweaty women in tight assed yoga pants."

"I never noticed. Is there a question here?"

"Does adjusting all those 'down dogs' make you horny?"

"No."

"Are you sure you're not gay?"

"Yep. Positive."

"What's the craziest thing you've seen in a yoga class?"

"Transformation."

"Transfor...what?!"

"Transformation."

"What's that have to do with yoga?"

"Everything."

A journey that began decades earlier for me at the request of my future ex-wife, Michelle.

"Yoga will be good for us." I knew when she said 'us,' she meant me. I met her challenge. A small, dark, desperate place inside an old single-story office building with worn carpeted floors, thick drapes over windows, and dozens of candles flickering wildly. All of this blanketed in a heavy smoke of burning sage. Just another cave. A cave full of people searching. I wandered deeper. Groping in the darkness. Transformation is what I found there entirely unexpectedly or accidentally on purpose.

My phone buzzes, interrupting my train of thought.

"Good morning, sunshine!" A text from Greta.

She is insufferable, needy, clingy, and a wet blanket of smothering. The complete package. The complete package of everything I didn't want. We began seeing each other by accident. She pursued, and I recoiled. She continued her assault, and I gave way either out of admiration for her dedication or my desperate need for a distraction.

"How are you this morning, handsome?"

I imagine the unpleasant sound of her voice as I read her text. Gratingly high-pitched airy, like knives sharpened on glass. Could she actually be speaking straight from the bridge of her nose?

"Morning," I text half-heartedly and instantly regret my reply.

"So what do you have planned for us this weekend?"

How do you say, 'I'd rather have my fingernails pulled out one by one than have to see you this weekend,' without sounding rude? Knowing that she hated being outdoors, I toss out, "Let's go kayaking."

A long pause.

"You know I don't want to do that! Come over to my place, and I'll make you a nice dinner."

It was a trap. Greta's idea of a nice dinner consisted of a frozen pizza and bagged salad, washed down with cheap red wine. Just her way to get me to her place so she could crush me on her couch while her dog Fritz dry humped my leg. Woman and beast, both powerless to my charm.

I loathed time on her couch. It was more of a brutally savage wrestling match than a precursor to pleasurable sex. Her foreplay was overly aggressive. Poking, squeezing, twisting, pulling, like being beaten with a bag of unripe oranges while standing in an automatic car wash set to sanitize. Getting it from all sides all at once. I always wanted to tap out, never seduced. It showed, and the conversation would devolve.

"What's wrong? Are you not into me?"

"No, I'm into you." I lied, knowing that pieces of my heart were somewhere else, with someone else.

"It's just it is hard to concentrate with Fritz licking my ass and humping my leg." A half-truth.

"FRITZ!!" she screeched.

Poor Fritz. Why do people always feel the need to yell at animals? I felt for him. He didn't want my pity or care about Greta's yelling. As far as it concerned him, she could yell until her nose fell off her face. His singular focus was my leg. I admired his determination. So, like an olive branch, I stretched out my leg to him and nodded toward it with approval. Message received. He took his position and eagerly began humping.

"FRITZ!!"

"Maybe. I've got a busy weekend of teaching ahead. I'm not sure how much energy I'll have," I say, trying hard not to commit.

"You always say that."

"It's true. I have all my regular classes plus a private lesson with a new client. Would you rather I lie to you?"

"No. I just want to see you."

"Ok, I'll let you know," remaining noncommittal. "Be

safe," I say, meant for me, not her.

That should keep her quiet for a little while.

I need some solitude. Click. The phone turned to 'do not disturb.' Dressed. I need a long walk in the woods to clear my head. A much-needed forest bath or *shinrin-yoku,* as the Japanese call it. Look how fancy I think I am. I shuffle through songs to find a new distraction. AURORA's very somber and stripped-down version of Bowie's 'Life on Mars' plays. The suitcase sound of the electric piano chimes against the whispery, pixyish vocals. What a way to set the tone for today's bath. I'm out the door.

Oh man! Look at those cavemen go
It's the freakiest show

Painfully, like swallowing thousands of tiny metal needles, the bitter cold, dry morning air enters my lungs. A few deep breaths and the pain subsides. I find the trail behind the apartment building that leads into the woods. I enter an amazing patch of preserved forest smack in the middle of mega-million-dollar home suburbia—a spiritual green oasis inside a soulless cultural wasteland.

Deeper in the woods, I'm alone again. It's darker here. The air is colder, untainted, and sticky—a drastic change from my claustrophobic cave home. Through gray winter skies, a mix of hardwood and southern pine trees stretch upwards, reaching for the sun. I move along a well-trafficked path, becoming lost in the music and thought.

Now she walks through her sunken dream

Sunken dream. So, so many sunken dreams. I fight it, but my mind moves to memories of Nicole. My body begins to uncontrollably retch and ache. I pause. Crouch down to catch my breath and try to hold back raw surging emotion. I feel the presence of my father: his leer and his judgment.

"What is wrong with you?!"

"Can't you see I'm in pain?"

"Pain? You're soft. You know nothing about pain."

"Thanks, Dad."

"Don't behave supercilious with me, son."

Spoken like the true red-blooded knuckle-dragging barbarian with a 25-cent vocabulary that he is.

"You're bent out of shape because a woman broke your heart? That's not pain. That's just you being effete. Women are like buses; a new one comes along every 15 minutes."

"Effete? Someone has been doing his crossword puzzles. For your information, I'm not looking for a bus."

"Don't get persnickety with me! Did I tell you about the time my stepfather beat me with a frying pan?"

"Yeah, Dad—you did. Not to get too persnickety, but did I ever tell you about the time my father threw me into a brick wall because I wouldn't eat my lima beans?"

The crowd goes quiet.

Oh man! Look at those cavemen go

Leaves stir. Tree limbs gently twist and snap. Tender footsteps on the forest floor. I'm not alone. Holding still, I focus my stare. Deer. Unaware of me, half a dozen of them appear slowly through the dense tree line and move in my direction. With calm grace, they stop to nibble on something in the leaves. My pain and the voice of my father are gone. A doe spots me. She continues chewing but watches me with a curious eye.

"I mean you no harm," I assure her in my mesmerized state of wonder. We trade stares for a few more seconds until from further down the trail, a man yells "DEER!!" and with that, they dart away. Spiraling on their hind legs and with two quick hops, their white-furred tails erect, they disappear back inside the safety of the tree line.

"Did you see those deer?!" exclaims the obese, red-faced yeller.

"You mean those deer you scared off?"

"Yeah, but I didn't scare them off!" He declares through shallow gasps of mouth breathing.

I shrug my shoulders as I move past him along the trail. Responsibility. No one ever takes any.

Oh man, wonder if he'll ever know
He's in the bestselling show
Is there life on Mars?

CHAPTER 3

"Inhale. Send your right leg high and point the toe." I've probably said this a million times. Now, it's a million and one. Back in my natural habitat—a yoga studio. A room full of sweaty bodies moving to my every command. The power could intoxicate, but it doesn't. I can't stand these people. They are pathetic. They aren't practicing the discipline of yoga. They are just exercising and nothing more. It insults me. They just like the word 'yoga' because it makes them feel special.

"Well, I got the cutest new yoga mat last week. It matches my yoga pants and everything. I get so sweaty in yoga! Namaste! Hehehe."

It's not their fault. It's my fault. Yoga, something that once gave me so much hope and happiness, had now become a prison of my own design. Too many painful memories attached to it. Too many thoughts of Nicole and our time together—teaching and practicing together. Now with her gone, I am left with the remains. I throw those remains at my students with disdain and anger.

"Be the light! Goddamit!" A TV cliché teacher, everything I resisted, I had become.

"Be. Here. Now."

"Where are you?"

"I'm where I need to be."

"Seems like you're obsessed with the past."

"Do as I say, not as I do. I'm the guru!"

I wasn't obsessed with the past so much as chained to it. I pulled at the links in the shackles. I fumbled with the lock, but I couldn't find a way to break free.

Through the studio's sound system and eerily right on cue, Coldplay's 'Yellow' with its acoustic intro and try-too-hard power pop dynamics fill the space. I really must stop letting my students pick the songs for my classes.

Look at the stars
Look how they shine for you
And everything you do
Yeah, they were all yellow

I never thought this was a great track, but I respect its pop sensibilities. I probably could do without all the over-the-top falsetto vocals, though. Regardless of my opinions, it brings back difficult memories.

Years earlier, I had swerved off the path. A broken body led to a broken mind, which led to a complete disconnect between the discipline of yoga and myself. I was rudderless. Hoping to heal me and my practice, I decided to recertify my teaching credentials. I arrived late into the room of other souls, each trying to find their way back to the path. The room was full of people and their nervous apprehension. Bodies packed like sardines in a can. I found a sliver of space to unroll my mat and began my standard warm-up routine. Shirshasana for eight minutes. Not showing off, just attempting to find calm in all the apprehension. After about six minutes, I hear a voice.

"Hey, can you move over so I can squeeze in?"

Somewhat annoyed, I slowly, without a hurry, make my way down to the floor. Without looking up, I move my mat to one side.

"Thanks."

I nod.

Back into my headstand, from the corner of my eye, I finally see her. She unrolls her mat next to me. Green yoga pants, matching tank top, and mat are all Lululemon. Arrggghh. The uniform of fake yogis everywhere—the fucking worst. Her stern face surrounded by straight strawberry blonde hair pulled back into a tight ponytail with short bangs up-front, punctuated with a nose ring. Oh, look, a forearm tattoo too—the dictionary definition of a cliché.

"I bet she's a real bitch," I thought to myself.

I was in love.

Your skin

Oh yeah, your skin and bones

Turn into something beautiful

You know, you know I love you so

You know I love you so

I hate you, Chris Martin, I genuinely do.

Back in the cave, attempting to make dinner. It's too late to be eating dinner. Anyone who tells you that the business of transforming lives is easy and requires no sacrifices has no idea at all. The long hours are taking their toll on me. The travel to studio after studio attempting to be physically and mentally ready for each class is draining. Afterward, students wanting to have deep intellectual conversations or just offload their issues onto me like a shade tree shrink is more than I can bear. Listen, but never offer advice is my mantra. But the stress is getting to me. I am withering. My body, leaner and leaner with each day. The fortitude of my mind constantly challenged. An unwilling contestant in an impossible juggling act, I am dropping balls.

My phone buzzes. Who is it now?

"Have I mentioned how horny I am for you? Just sayin'."

Well, that's subtle... 'Just sayin.' Doesn't anyone start with a 'hello' anymore? It's Dani. An old girlfriend from my high school years. We talked over coffee a few times since she found me on social media a while ago. I was being friendly. She clung to the past. It was awkward. She told me she never stopped loving me. I changed the subject. As before, it was awkward.

"I've been thinking about you all day," she continues.

"Hello," I reply. Let's act like civilized people.

"Oh, hi. Have you been thinking about me?"

No, I say to myself.

"It's been a busy day. Haven't had a second to stop." I don't have the heart to tell her no.

Her husband loved cocaine more than his wife and daughters. He hid his habit. The stress of life was just too much for him, I suppose. We all deal with it in our own way. After filling his nose one too many times, he landed himself in an ICU bed in a coma with permanent brain damage. All of Dani's tears and yelling couldn't save him. He slowly drifted back to Earth. Too many hearts broken at once.

"How long will that take?"

"To break a heart? Seconds."

Understandably, she was an emotional wreck, but I didn't have the tools to mend her. Holding myself together was hard enough. I needed a friend. She wanted a do-over. There's no such thing.

"Would you come over and fuck me?"

Less subtle. The last time we had sex was two decades ago. So, I'm unsure where all of this is coming from so soon. All I want to do is to eat my dinner and go to bed, but I rarely get what I want.

"I'm just getting home and grabbing something to eat. Can I take a rain check?"

Nothing says 'I'm really not that into you' like asking for a 'sex rain check.'

"Ok... I'm still soooo horny. Can we play over the phone?" with wink emoji added for greater impact.

Accidentally typing, "Sure," when I meant to type, "No." What's the worst that can happen?

"Want to FaceTime?"

Some faces don't need time.

"Nah, it'd be sexier just hearing your voice."

My phone rings. It's Dani. I answer. She's moaning. She started without me. I grab my food and head to my bedroom. In the bed, I catch the sound of bedsheets moving along with her moans and whispers. I instantly feel sick to my stomach. It isn't because of the food.

"Are you naked?" she asks.

"Yes." I wasn't.

"Are you hard?"

"Yes, very." I wasn't.

"Hmmm. I'm going to come."

Already? I just got here. Why is everyone is in such a hurry?

"OHHHHHHH!!!"... and she's done.

"Your turn, baby," an exhausted Dani whispers.

So, *this* is the worst that can happen.

"Oh, I came earlier," I mumble between bites of food. I hadn't. We say our goodnights. One of us will sleep soundly tonight.

I finish my food. Set my plate on the nightstand, take off my t-shirt, and lean back into the pillows. Stretching out on the bed, I'm exhausted. When you fall apart, everyone scrambles for a piece they always have. Is the entire world replete with nothing more than ill-intended self-absorbed individuals whose only purpose in life is to use me? Their intention to pick over the best parts of my life like a morbidly obese, thumb-fingered uncle does with a Christmas ham. Licking their fingers, with nothing left of me to consume, they hit the exit door looking for another life to gorge themselves on. My disdain for the human race grows.

The front door opens. "Come on in," Mike's voice slurs—he's not alone. I hear two young female voices too. Two prostitutes? Mike, you can barely handle one for more than 120 seconds. Now you want to add a second? My friend, you might want to pace yourself. I listen closer. No, these aren't prostitutes. They are young. Their speech is slurred and loose. I can hear them stumble and laugh uncontrollably. They're high or drunk—probably both. A true professional is never both at the same time.

"Make yourselves some drinks and don't break anything. I'll be right back." Mike says as he closes the front door, leaving our new house guests alone.

"Does someone else live here too?"

"Yeah. I think he's a yoga teacher or something like that. You should get with him. You need more yoga in your life. I bet he's into that tantra stuff too. The sex would be like amazing."

A bottle crashes onto the hardwood floors—the sound of liquid mixed with shards of glass pelts the walls. High-pitched laughter erupts.

"Enough!" I mumble to myself as I jump out of bed to investigate. Opening the bedroom, I find two unattractive young girls standing shoeless in a puddle of champagne. A ragged and sweaty-looking dirty blonde girl looks at the floor in tragic disbelief while her cohort, a dumpy brunette in thigh-high cut denim shorts, laughs uncontrollably.

"Hello, ladies," I say calmly.

The laughing stops.

"What happened here?" I ask.

"She dropped the bottle of champagne that we just got," says the brunette through drunken hiccups.

"Now, what are we going to drink?" chimes in the sweaty one still looking at the floor.

"That's no big deal. There's another bottle in the fridge. A student gave it to me. You can have it. I won't drink it."

"Really?!" they say in unison.

"Really."

Without regard for the glass on the floor, they both make their way to the refrigerator like two mindless moths to a flickering lightbulb. Door opened. Bottle found. Cork popped. The champagne flows into empty juice glasses. All is right with the world again.

"Happy now?"

"Yes!"

"By the way, I'm Ian."

Looking up from their glasses for the first time, they realize that I'm standing there shirtless. Their eyes pause on my naked chest before looking at my face.

"I'm Courtney, and this is Kristy," says the brunette, pointing her glass at the sweaty one.

"Nice to meet you. Where'd Mike go?"

"Who?" asks Courtney.

"Mike. The guy that let you in."

"Oh, yeah, Mike," Kristy says laughingly to Courtney as she moves across the room towards me. "Yeah, I'm not sure, but do you want to drink with us?" landing her hand on my forearm, drawing herself closer to me.

"Probably not. I was just heading to bed before I heard the bottle shatter."

Kristy, with her hand still on my forearm, ignoring my comment, looks into my eyes to ask, "Are you circumcised?"

Subtlety is truly a lost art.

"I'm sorry but isn't finding out for yourself part of the fun?" I play along.

"I *do* want to find out for myself," she offers with a crooked smile and wrinkle of her nose.

"I bet you do," I say teasingly. "Thanks, but I just came." I hadn't. I pull her arm off mine and say, "I'm going to bed. Watch yourself with all of that glass on the floor. Feel free to clean it up too. Goodnight."

Kristy stands slackjawed and speechless as I move

away from her and back to my room. I flop face down into the dirty sheets. I'm exhausted again. Sleep comes, but it's nothing more than just another tease.

In the morning, the winter sun weakly forces its way through the window blinds. I'm awake again, but just enough to chase the dreams away. My first thought is of Nicole, and my heart sinks. Suddenly realizing that I'm lingering there too long, I pull back the sheets. Standing, I feel my feet on the floor. They are sore, heavy, and weary. I feel depleted before the day has even begun. I present an offering of water and incense that accompanies my morning 'thank yous.' Pathetic and meager.

"Are you going to meditate? It's been so long since you tried," I dig at myself.

"You must be joking."

Meditation, like sleep, had become sporadic and broken. Something that was once so fulfilling, so gratifying, had devolved into an internal battlefield and emotional blood bath. Any positive ground covered was instantly lost two-fold to thoughts of regret, loneliness, and or heartbreak. The basic idea of attempting to sit still with my own thoughts made me physically ill. I had lost the plot. My grip was surely slipping. Distractions, distractions, and more distractions were my only remedy.

If you twist and turn away
If you tear yourself in two again
If I could, yes, I would
If I could, I would

U2's 'Bad' lands to my ears like a swift kick to the shins. Yep, these are easy. I twisted, turned, and tore myself in two again and again. I twisted, contorted to the point of breaking, only to become unrecognizable to myself. I turned the other cheek because this one is bruised beyond repair. Tearing and tearing at myself until there was almost nothing left.

Let it go

Surrender

Dislocate

The much harder parts.

In the kitchen for coffee and breakfast. The floor is sticky. It smells like dried alcohol and sweat. I guess the girls didn't feel free enough to clean up after themselves. No sign of Mike this morning, but the trash can full of empty bottles and broken glass tells me that the party must have continued long after I left. I wonder if he had sex with both of our clumsy guests last night. Honestly, I didn't want to know. I couldn't think much less of him anyhow. Who am I to judge what makes someone else happy?

I am wandering back into the woods. The sun gave up any attempt to break through the gray cloud cover above. The skies are heavy. A storm is coming; I can feel the pressure change. I find a new path. One I've never seen before. It takes me higher up into the hills. The climb is slippery through red clay, loose rocks, and exposed roots. The storm is in a hurry. The wind churns through the trees. The half thought of turning back is brushed away. Keep moving.

"Nothing happens when you're at a standstill. Keep moving. Backward or forward, you've got to keep moving," something I always told Nicole.

"What if I make the wrong decision?" she asked.

"You won't know if you don't move."

"Then what?"

"You learn. That's all you can do," I replied.

I'm not sure she ever really understood what I was trying to say. I never wanted to deprive her of the opportunity to learn. I never showed her the shortcut because there are none. I only ever wanted her to succeed and to be fulfilled in her journey.

If I could through myself
Set your spirit free, I'd lead your heart away
See you break, breakaway
Into the light
and into the day

Her dream of building a yoga studio stalled. She was reeling, but her ego wouldn't let it go. I did the only thing that I know how to do, help. I helped because I loved her even though I knew her vision would end in complete failure.

Almost to the top of the hill. The wind continues its assault here on dozens and dozens of eastern white pine trees. Dead. Consumed from the inside. All their hope and promise now dried black. Once a thriving and proud towering woodland of evergreens now stripped of their limbs, reduced to nothing more than a patch of tall toothpicks. A few cling to life, but their vitality wanes; the end is near. They wait, hoping for the winds to come and land their final blow, bringing them crashing down to the forest floor and out of their misery.

To let it go
And so to fade away
To let it go
And so, fade away

In a clearing, I find a seat to watch the exchange. The wind becomes punishing and unrelenting. Holding on by the fingers of their roots to the dense clay soil below, the hardwood trees bend, sway and bow to the wind's command. The sky transitions from coal-black to powdery white and back again. Rain-heavy clouds, ready to burst, convulse and swirl. Large patches of black bark break free from the pines and whip through the forest air. As the onslaught continues one by one, the dead pine bone spires begin to break and unceremoniously land with faint thuds. Back to the Earth again and again.

I am a ghost here, a powerless witness to the fury and chaos before me. Knowing all too well that I am ill-prepared for what is about to happen next, I still invite it to come. Let it come down. Let it all come down.

This desperation
Dislocation
Separation, condemnation
Revelation in temptation
Isolation, desolation
Let it go

CHAPTER 4

Exhausted and thoroughly depleted, I pull the car into the driveway. Press the P to park the car. My feet are sore from a day's worth of pacing. Being barefoot in hot, sweaty rooms all day has left me drained. The attempt to find the energy and motivation to remain positive and to teach positivity when I am anything but feels like a lie. It grates at me.

Sitting there, I take a moment to look at the house in front of me. A dark, single-story structure in a very nice suburban neighborhood. The wood siding painted a light brown. Small windows hidden below a low sloping roofline. Very modest and humble. The landscaping minimal and bare, dotted with large boulders that, while heavy, appear to float like ships in a harbor on the dormant winter grass. A single garden lamp in the center of the yard timdly emits a message with its dim flickering glow, 'We want the world to know that someone lives here, but we don't want any visitors.' I respect it.

Asha, the owner of the house, had contacted me a few weeks earlier inquiring about private instruction. After exchanging a few emails, we agreed on her choice of a very particular day and time to begin her lessons. I thought it unusual, but if it meant something to her, I was okay with it. I didn't know much about her. When she came to my classes, she was meek and timid. Always walking with her shoulders rolled forward, lost in thought. She never looked me in the eye when I greeted her or spoke a word to other students. I respect her solemnness but also thought teaching her might be a challenge.

I ring the doorbell. Another dim light comes on above the front door. I hear at least three locks unclick before the seal of the door is broken, revealing Asha. Another glass storm door that separates us has to be unlocked before I could say, "Hello."

"Hello. How are you?" Asha says while looking to the floor. "Please come in."

Inside, she asks me to remove my shoes. I kneel and untie them. She scurries across the dark hardwoods, grabbing a chair and some flip-flops.

"I'm so sorry," she apologizes as she pulls a chair towards me. "Please take a seat. Here are some chappals— I mean, sandals for you to wear too. I hope you don't mind."

"I'm fine. Please don't bother," I say while slipping on the chappals.

The interior of the house is dark and lifeless. A seventies-style contemporary bungalow with vaulted ceilings and exposed rough timber beams. Bare walls painted a pale yellow with white trim, and a few small pieces of art hung too high, making them appear miniature. Large, uncomfortable-looking pieces of ultra-modern European furniture wrapped in leather and chrome seem out of place.

From an adjoining room behind a half wall, the staccato sound of Enya's 'Orinoco Flow' comes blaring in so loudly that it makes my teeth hurt.

Noticing my discomfort, she says, "I'm so sorry. Let me turn this music down". She dashes into the other room. I can hear her fumble with a few controls, lowering the volume only a fraction of a decibel.

Returning with an embarrassing smile, "I'm so sorry. Such an inauspicious way for us to start my teaching journey with you."

"It's not a problem."

She is nervous. It is obvious. It looks like she lives alone, but I had seen her in my classes with a younger girl, which I assume is her daughter.

"Where is your daughter?"

"Oh, Ziya. She's with her father this weekend."

WE CAN SAIL, WE CAN SAIL
WE CAN STEER, WE CAN NEAR WITH ROB DICKINS
AT THE WHEEL

Enya continues to wail incessantly at the highest roar possible from the other room about sailing away. "I'm so sorry. That continues to be very loud. Let me turn that down some more." Back to the other room, she goes to fumble again with a knob or something.

"Don't worry, it's not a problem," I say as I open my jaw to pop my eardrum. "Shall we get started?"

"Will this be a suitable place for our lesson?" motioning to the room where Enya continued to scream about sailing.

"Sure. This room will be fine."

"Before we begin, I have a request, and it may sound strange."

"Ok."

"In my culture, we hold our teachers in very high regard. We like to honor them before each lesson. I would like to do that for you. Is this ok with you?"

"Ok," I say, apprehensively unsure about what was about to happen next.

"Thank you. Please remove your chappals. Er, your sandals. Excuse me. I meant to say your flip-flops. English is not my first language."

"That's ok. I understand," removing my chappals.

"Please stand here." Following her request, I move to the center of the room and stand in front of her. Kneeling in front of me, she kisses my bare feet.

In all my years of teaching, I thought I'd seen it all. A pair of sweaty ladies' yoga pants left on the hood of my car. A woman attending my class wearing a tennis skirt without panties. A student stalking me on social media to tell me she loved me. All of which were not gratifying moments for me as a teacher. This foot kissing thing, however, was different. Asha sees me as a true teacher of the discipline of yoga, not a cliché. It feels good. Odd, but still good.

Carry me on the waves to the lands I've never been,
Carry me on the waves to the lands I've never seen.

She finishes her kissing and says, "Ok, that is all. We can now continue with the lesson. Thank you for indulging me. I hope it wasn't too much to ask."

"No, not at all. Shall we begin?"

We spend the next hour discussing her connection to yoga along with her goals. Most people think of yoga as nothing more than a workout to make them sweat. Asha is different. She wants to focus on each posture's alignment and is not interested in fancy poses or bendy movements. She subscribes to my belief that the only reason we perform the physical practice is so we can sit still longer in meditation. After an hour or so, I pack my things to leave. She comments that she enjoyed the lesson and looked forward to the next one soon.

"Perhaps, if I'm not being too forward, you could come over one evening for dinner. I can make traditional Nepali food. Of course, this would be outside of lesson time. Would you like that?"

"Sure. That sounds nice," I say, but think, "Oh no, not another one."

"Splendid! I'll email you to arrange a day and time."

I say my goodbyes, leaving my chappals behind.

CHAPTER 5

Opening the front door to the cave, I instantly smell the musty odor of water. Did no one clean up the champagne yet? Those disgusting animals. Another sniff. It's not champagne. It is the stench of sitting water. The smell of water-soaked sheetrock walls, wet linens, waterlogged hardwood floors. With the lights on, I see it all. The ceiling drips with water in straight lines to the floor. Squish. The wood is soft under my feet. I see water oozing from between the seams in the floorboards. In my bedroom, the carpet is cold and wet beneath my feet. The morning's downpour had penetrated the roof three floors above and trickled its way to my bedroom. When I said that I wanted it to come down, this wasn't exactly what I meant.

Fortunately, most of my meager belongings were

hastily tossed into a storage unit when Nicole and I split. All that remains here are clothes, shoes, and a few books, now all thoroughly soaked and ruined. A nervous glance to the windowsill, my Buddha! My heart stops, believing that she is damaged too. The clothes and books are replaceable! Crossing the room in a single stride, I am next to her. No damage, not a single drop of water on her. I grab a towel, wrap her up tightly, and put her inside my backpack.

"Hey Mike, we have a problem. Call me," I text.

While I wait for his reply, my thoughts race. He owns this place; he's going to have to get it fixed ASAP. Where am I going to live in the meantime? Could things get any worse?

My phone rings.

"Hey, sorry about the mess. I'll get it cleaned up," Mike starts.

"You know about this?"

"The bottle of champagne that the girls dropped last night? Yeah, they were drunker than a bunch of skunks, but we sure did have some fun."

"I'm not talking about the champagne and the strippers. I'm talking about the water leaking from the ceiling," I fire back.

"First of all, they weren't strippers. Second, I don't know anything about any water damage."

"I don't care about their employment history or what's on their W2. I care that all my stuff is ruined. There's water running down the walls in my bathroom and bedroom. It's like an indoor water park here!"

"My papa would say, God, rest his soul, 'No use crying over spilled milk.' I'll get it fixed. Sorry. Hang in there." He hangs up.

"Hang in there," the nerve he has saying that to me. The prostitutes, drunks, champagne-covered floors, and now this. To borrow a phrase from Mike's Papa, "I'm hanging in there like loose teeth."

A slammed door wakes me from a fragile sleep. Even with my eyes open, I can't quite remember where I am in this jet-black dark. Where am I? I am a bit nervous but then suddenly realize I left Mike's apartment late last night in sheer frustrated exhaustion and checked myself into a hotel, and from the smell of it, not a very nice hotel at that.

"*I am here*," I declare. Humanity summed up in a single sentence.

I roll over and attempt to rebuild my rudely shattered slumber. It's futile. Whenever I am awake in bed, I think only of Nicole. The bed is too big without her. I miss her warmth. The way she nestled her head on my shoulder and fell asleep. I miss her so.

After six weeks of teacher training, constant conversations about our passion for yoga, and her dream of opening her own studio, we had become inseparable. A deep connection that we both felt had arrived for both of us. The problem was that we were both unhappily married. One day she sent me a text telling me that she'd filed for divorce.

"We just want different things," she said. "I'm done."

I was shocked and somewhat jealous of her impulsive, carefree attitude, especially to a marriage of 8 years. I didn't possess those qualities. My loyalty is faulty, but I thought of her differently after she told me about her decision. Could we have a future as a couple? I caught myself fantasizing about it more than a few times. Impossible! She's 27, and I'm 44. It'll never happen. I tried to chase the dream of us together away, but as a lost dog, it kept coming back. I tried not to feed it, but it was curled up in my lap and wouldn't leave.

One morning, after a fitful sleep of chasing the dog, I screwed up the nerve and sent her a text.

"Let's meet for lunch. I want to take you to this Buddhist temple. You'll love it."

Within seconds, her reply: "Yes!"

We met for lunch at a hip, sterile, ultra-modern Asian bistro. We chatted over oily braised cabbage, steamed rice, and yellow-curried tofu skins. Mostly about yoga, the studio she was building, and her divorce.

"I want you to teach for my studio. You'd be a great addition," she said.

"Sure. Sounds fun," I distractedly replied. Not knowing what I had just agreed to, I had other things on my mind. We finished our food and sipped on milk teas with black tapioca pearls. I was nervous about those other things on my mind.

I clumsily blurted out, "Hey, I know that this might sound strange, but... well, I rarely do this... I believe we have a connection, and I'd like to explore that connection with you. I mean, we both like each other. Am I wrong?" Smooth.

The expression in her eyes told me I was right, but she couldn't find the words. So, she smiled, fiddled with her chopsticks, and paused while she searched for what to say.

"Um, yeah, I'm into you too, but..."

I hate 'buts.'

"... I'm just getting divorced, and aren't you married? So maybe we just hit the pause button until we both get our shit figured out? Let's just be friends."

It ruined me. How could we be friends, or I teach for her studio after that kind of rejection?

"My wife gave up on me and us years ago. My marriage is dead. Let me sort that out," I said reservedly. "Now I feel like an idiot."

"Don't. I really like you. I just need to process some things about my marriage, but I don't want us to stop being friends."

Awkward pause.

"I get it. Do you still want to go to the temple today, or will that be weird?"

"Yes, let's do it," she replied.

At the temple, a converted church of God, we said our thanks in our socks, made our offerings to a 30-foot golden gilded Buddha, and sat in silence. It was peaceful, despite the embarrassment that I had just suffered over lunch. Bernard Montgomery, Scipio Africanus, and Shaka Zulu all suffered significant losses, I'm sure. But I bet my last dollar that they were never humiliated over a glass of bubble tea like I was today. I said my many 'thank yous' again, and I gave myself credit for offering my truth to Nicole. I'd live to fight another day and was proud of myself. My father would say, "You don't want to die with regrets and/or while wearing dirty underwear." I agree with half of that statement.

After leaving the temple, we spent the day in the Spanish part of the city drinking Café con Leches and eating Sopaipillas in a tiny, family-run café. Later we strolled through dimly lit, empty aisles of a Supermercado trying on straw hats, having serious conversations about what our dream piñata would be filled with, and bought a few Veladoras Religiosas with an image of Our Lady of Guadalupe on them.

It was getting late, so I drove her back to her car. We sat in the empty restaurant parking lot, laughing about the day while we watched a drunk woman yell at an empty trashcan tipped on its side. I don't remember what I said, but it must have landed just right. So, in my German car with its smooth leather seats, under the faint flicker of the parking lot lights, while the drunk hurdled obscenities at the quiescent trashcan, we kissed. The world drifted by, and we kissed again. In that instant, that most precious moment, the universe took control of me, and I became lost in her.

"No regrets, Dad. No regrets."

Another door slams with a crash.

"Does anyone know how to close a door here?" I half yell to no one in particular.

I fumble for my phone. It's off. I turn it on. I overslept. It instantly vibrates with new messages.

Greta: "Hey handsome, am I gonna see you tonight?"

Dani: "I'm naked. Do you want to come over? I'm waiting."

Mike: "The water stopped leaking. It's going to take a few days to fix. I'm having drinks with Kristy and Courtney tonight. You should meet us, or we can come to your hotel. Hang in there."

Asha: "I hope it is not too forward of me, but I was wondering if you would like to join me for dinner tomorrow night at my home. I'll be making traditional

Nepali food. Nothing fancy. Please feel free to say no."

It's hard to know where to begin with these messages, so I don't and toss the phone back on the bed. Roll onto my back and stare blankly at the ceiling. My feet ache, and they haven't even touched the floor. So, this is what everything at once feels like. Is it better than the alternative?

I'm in no hurry to face a day of everything. I create a crude alter for Buddha on the desk among all its notepads, pens, and colorful brochures. Brew a horrid cup of coffee that I promptly pour down the toilet. Say my late morning 'thank yous,' sans an offering, and jump back between the coarse plastic flower-covered bedspread and fibrous starch-white sheets. Basic extreme comfort awaits. I scroll through the day's news to see that it's all about the virus. How have I missed all this? Assuring myself that this is nothing to worry about, I doze off to sleep again.

I wake up after lunch. Decide to try the day again.

To Greta: "Unsure. I've got a bunch of classes to teach today, and my place flooded a few days ago. I'll let you know."

To Dani: "Probably not. Enjoy your day."

To Mike: "Ok. Keep me posted. I have plans tonight. Tell the girls I say hello. What do you make of this virus that the news is talking about?"

To Asha: "Yes, sounds nice. Should I bring something?"

Morning texts sent. Into a long, hot shower. The Bunnymen's 'Cutter' melody arrives in my head, and I can't escape its tribal rhythmic pounding and vocal howlings.

Conquering myself
Until I see another hurdle approaching

Say we can say we will
Not just another drop in the ocean

Conquering myself sounds like some perverse version of self-flagellation, but I know it's not. I understand that the only path to my happiness is to conquer myself, my ego, and to let go of my attachments. On its face, happiness seems to be a modern human problem. Generations have come and gone without the slightest notion of it. My father never understood what the word meant.

"You get married to a moderately attractive woman that can cook. Work at a job for the next 40 years that you hate. Spend all your money on things you don't need and come home to a child that would rather spit on you than love you. Forget about your happiness. It doesn't exist." Such inspiring words for a father to impart on his son at the tender age of 15. He could have just simply punched me in the groin and said, "Welcome to the world; you're going to hate it here." It would have arrived with the same frigid apocalyptic optimism.

He resigned to hating his life, which explained the anger that boiled inside the inferno of his desolate and lonely soul. Left unregulated, it mutated from an unorthodox absolution to raw polluted violence, whose only target was a wife that couldn't cook and a child that neither loved nor hated him. His addiction to brutality bordered on sadism.

Opening his bedroom closet doors: "So which will it be, son? The dress shoe, the leather belt, or the hand?" he asked with a wanton sickness in his smile. So many options for an eight-year-old child to choose from, a Marquis de Sade's basement of sorts, but for children. Welcome to Sadists 'R Us. "Consider yourself lucky there are kids in China that don't have this many choices."

"The hand. I *want* the hand," I said with full-throated determination. I wanted him to feel it too.

Skin meets skin with a thunderous clap. Pain arrives, the room goes black.

> *Am I the happy loss*
> *Will I still recoil*
> *When the skin is lost*
> *Am I the worthy cross*
> *Will I still be soiled*
> *When the dirt is off*

With the dirt washed off but I still feel soiled. Will I still recoil?

My phone buzzes to life from the bedroom.

Asha: "Splendid! No need to bring a thing. See you at 8?"

Resisting the urge to climb back into bed, I get dressed to leave my minuscule and bleak rented room.

CHAPTER 6

"Trust yourself. Explore new things and learn. From Adho Mukha Svanasana, bend your knees, press the weight into your hands, and move forward into Adho Mukha Vrksasana. Nicely done. Move back to Adho Mukha Svanasana and vinyasa."

I'm in the worst place in the world—a hot yoga class. The dynamic is different here; I'm not the teacher but a student. Hearing the words 'trust yourself' sounds so contrived and pretentious. What does this person who's been practicing 'yoga' for less than 18 months know about "trusting yourself"? I spent my entire life refusing to suffer phonies. I always regret coming but continue to arrive at this studio in secret four times a week to practice my asanas in anonymity. I'm here as an act of contrition, only to beat myself up physically as another means of distraction. It might be more gratifying to beat myself with an electrical extension cord. Maybe I'm here to listen to someone else talk, even if their scripted drivel sounds uninspiringly trite. Having another voice in my head shuts up my own brutal internal discourse.

"The light in me sees and honors the light in you," the teacher drones. Nonsense! I almost gag on the corniness of this non-believable self-help rubbish.

I roll up my mat and towel off my body. Grabbing my things, I meekly head through the chic studio lobby without saying goodbye and out the door into a dark, rainy winter afternoon. Idling in the car with the engine running, I wait for the heat to arrive. I see my yoga teacher burst into the parking lot from my rearview mirror, moving with angry animation. Her face red with fury, her jaw moving like a pit bull attacking a rotisserie chicken—she's enraged. I roll down my window to hear what she's saying.

"You scratched my car, you fucking idiot!" she says accusingly to a man helplessly frozen in shock. "What is wrong with you? You are going to pay for this!"

I feel for the alleged accidental vandal but laugh at the hysterical yoga teacher. 'The light in me sees the idiot in you that scratched my car.' Trust yourself, huh? That's rich.

As my phone buzzes, I turn my attention away from the comical karmic bloodbath that's taking place behind me.

Dani: "Why do you keep pushing me off? I thought you were into me."

"Sorry, I've been really busy. I'm about to teach a class now. Do you want to meet me tomorrow morning?" I text.

Dani: "Yes!"

I'm confident that she wouldn't be that enthusiastic about things after tomorrow. I'd already made my mind up about Dani. I needed to let her go. She's too aggressive. I know she wants more from me than I am willing to give. I thought I was being nice by keeping her at arm's length, but she isn't taking the hint. I don't want to hurt her. God knows that she's been through enough, but it's time for radical measures. The least I can do is tell her in person; tomorrow seems like a million years away.

Walking into the studio to teach my last class of the day, I receive a text from Mike, "The place is all dried out. The contractor said he'll be finished with repairs in two days. When everything is done, the girls are coming over to party! The virus thing is a joke!" A good news/bad news scenario. Good news, I can check out of my dismal hotel room; bad news, I get to check back into my equally awful cave with all its constant distractions of "entertainment." I attempt to find a bright side to all of this, but nothing comes to mind.

I sleepwalk through another class. So bored with my students and their lack of dedication. How many times must I say the same things and they not get it? I stick around to answer a few moronic questions about this evening's class.

"So, in triangle pose. Where should I be feeling it?"

"Are you a supermodel?" I say dead-faced.

"Um, no," a confused student replies.

"So, why do you call it a 'pose'? For future reference, it's Trikonasana or Utthita Trikonasana, not 'triangle,'" said with a gallon of cutting venom. I'm almost certain they can sense my disdain for them in my body language alone. Opening my mouth only confirms what they already know. I pack my things and hurriedly leave with no real place to go.

Back in my seedy motel room, sitting on the floor eating Thai takeout, I watch the news. There's lots of discussion and panic about the virus and how people all over the world are getting sick and dying. Who mixes tomato, watered-down peanut butter, half-cooked noodles with baby corn and calls it 'Pad Thai'? I can't tell if I'm eating noodles or the Styrofoam box it came in. The box probably has more nutritional value. Entirely inedible. I hate to see it go to waste. I open the door and leave the container on the hallway floor. Maybe the rats will eat it. I have my doubts as I climb into bed.

A knock on the door. I ignore it and roll over. Again, more knocks and louder this time.

"Who is it?" I growl face down in the pillow.

"It's Dani, baby. Don't you remember that I was coming over this morning?"

"Yeah, hold on."

Is it tomorrow already? I'm out of bed. Into a pair of sweatpants and unlock the door.

"Morning."

"Hiya. Long night last night?" Dani says with a warm smile.

"Yeah, I guess. I don't remember falling asleep."

"You must have been out of it. You sent me a text last night telling me where you were staying."

"I did?" I say, somewhat confused.

She looks down at the hallway floor to last night's Thai leftovers. The Styrofoam box is chewed and shredded; the orange mess of noodles inside remains untouched.

"I knew it!" I blurt out loud with my suspicions confirmed.

"Is that yours?" Dani pointed to the box.

"Nah, that's for my pet rat. He's a picky eater. Do you want to come in?"

"Sure."

"Can I make you some coffee? I'll warn you now; it's disgusting."

"Ok," she agrees without considering the question. "Can I use your bathroom?"

"Yeah," I say from the coffee pot while pointing to the door.

I brew a dreadful cup of coffee in the cheap black plastic single-serve coffee maker. Turn my attention to the Buddha, offer her a fresh cup of water, and my morning gratitudes. I give her an extra thank you for the strength she's given me as I prepare to let Dani down easy.

With my eyes still closed in thought, I hear the toilet flush and the bathroom door open.

"Whatcha doing?" Dani asks.

I open my eyes, still focused on the serene statue in front of me. "It's my morning routine. Just offering my thanks."

"Ahh, ok. So you're praying."

"Nope, not exactly," I turn to look at her. She is standing naked in the doorway. To say it shocked me would be a lie; she's always been about as tactful as a land mine. It's been 25 years since I last saw her naked. The years collected their toll on her with interest. Her body pasty white, skin slack, littered with pockmarks like a plastic kitchen bag filled with three-week old cottage cheese. She's tall, so she doesn't look fat. Rubenesque would be an excellent way to describe her. A body covered with ill-advised tattoos. On her right shoulder is a clumsy, amateurish poor man's copy of *The Great Wave of Kanagawa* by Hokusai. Above the crease of her sagging breasts is a script tattoo that says 'Love Me, All of Me.' Subtle.

"What's going on?" I ask after scanning her body.

"I want you to fuck me. That's what is going on," she says bluntly.

"What do you take in your coffee?" I let the comment fly by me and walk to the coffeemaker.

"I just want you," she continues with explosive rawness.

"Yeah, I got that. Please put some clothes on, and let's talk."

"Are you going to fuck me?" she says with her hands on her hips.

"We'll see. Just put some clothes on."

She returns from the bathroom, returning this time in a red sleeveless dress dotted with tiny white flowers. It makes her body appear more angular than it is. She looks cute like I remembered her when we were young. Sitting down at the end of the bed, her dress clashes loudly with the muted pink and orange colors of the crumpled synthetic bedspread. I hand her a coffee and begin brewing another cup for myself.

"I know we just reconnected. It's great to see you and talk to you again after all these years," I begin, "but I have to be honest with you."

Anxiety arrives in her pale blue eyes like a hurricane. She sits still, quietly listening while sipping on the scalding hot brown water.

"I don't want to give you the wrong idea, but I'm not ready to be in a relationship. My life is too messed up right now. I can't be what you want."

Silence. More sipping of the hot dirt brown water is the stall tactic of the nervous.

"I thought we found each other at just the right time in our lives when we needed each other the most," she says, fighting through the storm of emotions. "I put you on a pedestal all those years ago. I built the steps to that pedestal, hoping that you'd come back to me. I always loved you."

"I know it seemed serendipitous, us meeting again after all these years but honestly," I pause, unsure if I want to say the next sentence out loud. "Honestly, I'm still in love with someone else. My heart is decimated." The truth.

Her anxiety turns to sadness, while her eyes become bloodshot, the color of her dress and fill with tears. She looks down at the cup of coffee in her trembling hands. Her face blushes while her body shudders in uncontrollable fits, spilling the brown sludge all over her fresh cotton dress and hands as she cries. Truth colliding with unrequited love is a cruel car crash. I did nothing but bear witness.

"Does she know?"

I was lost in thought. "I'm sorry, what did you say?"

"Does she know that you still love her? You need to tell her. You MUST tell her. She needs to know. If you truly love her, you will tell her," she implores.

Her absolute selflessness shocks me. "I've tried. She won't talk to me."

"Don't give up," she stares at me through a deluge of tears.

A knock on the door.

"Who is it?" I yell.

"It's hotel maintenance. There's something wrong with your heater; I am here to check it out."

I open the door to see a stout black man with fat fingers wearing a yellow safety vest and sunglasses, "Hello, yeah, now is not a good time. Can you come back later?" Looking over my shoulder back to Dani.

"Sorry, sir, my boss said I had to fix the heater right this second. It'll be just a few minutes."

"Yeah, now is not a good time. Come back later."

"Sorry, sir, my boss said to do it now. So I'm here to do it now."

"Ok," I say reluctantly, opening the door to let him enter.

He walks past Dani, who continues to cry, and acknowledges her with a "ma'am" as he heads to the window unit. He tinkers with the control panel. The unit cranks up with a loud whirring hiss, then promptly shuts off. He firmly raps the tan metal panel with his knuckles. Nothing changed.

"Hmmm?" he says and turns another set of knobs. It blows with a repetitive clicking noise and stops like a breathless old man who just ran a half marathon while smoking a pack of cigarettes. More tapping ensues before he declares with straight-faced confidence, "Well, it's constantly inconsistent."

I laugh at his astute diagnosis. "Aren't we all?" I reply with snarky confidence.

"I'm gonna need to order some parts. I don't know how long it will take." Spoken like the truly sacred mantra of every repairman since the dawn of things that needed fixing.

"No worries. It takes as long as it takes," I say, trying to hurry him out.

"Sir, you seem like a very cool and chill fellow. You've got good energy—a free spirit."

"Thanks. It's nice to believe that at least one person in this room thinks that," I say, looking at Dani with a crooked smile. She just stares at the floor, hiding her tears and blood-red eyes.

The repairman heads to the door, and with disgust, he looks down at the noodles on the hall floor, sitting bare with almost no Styrofoam remaining.

"Sir, is this your food?"

"No," I lie.

"You know people should stop feeding these rats."

"Why?"

"Because the world is coming to an end, that's why. These rats spread disease. The end days are here."

"End days for rats?" I play with him.

"End days for all of God's creatures! God will have his reckoning," he says like a half-believable, snake-handling faith healer.

"Hmmm. Speaking of consistently inconsistent," I snap back with a smile and rolling eyes.

"You shouldn't mock God, sir."

"I'll do my best. Appreciate you," I offer without meaning it and abruptly close the door in his face.

When I return to the room, I find that Dani has collected her things and poured the remaining coffee into the bathroom sink.

"Are you leaving?" I ask.

"Yes, there's really nothing left to say, is there?"

"I guess not," somewhat relieved. "I just wanted to be honest with you and not lead you on. Are you going to be ok?"

"Yes, I'll be fine. Thank you," she says half-heartedly and unconvincingly.

We hold an awkwardly firm hug for a few minutes too long, and then she's gone.

"Take care of yourself," I mumble with a sympathetic smile. As I close the door, I think, "Well, that was easier than I had imagined." Selfishly, I'm relieved. No yelling. No insults. No imaginative name-calling. Just acceptance. Don't we all actively seek and desire truth but lack the fundamental ability to handle it when it arrives? Certainly, she must have known that things would end this way.

"You can't give up today for the promises of what tomorrow might bring," I say out loud, only in an attempt to make myself feel better. It fails. "Nothing lasts forever." That's more the spirit.

CHAPTER 7

I'm wandering on a different path now—a well-worn pathway that embraces the shrug of the hills. Water from the slope above trickles through channels in the dirt to collect in pools of rich, overly-trodden black mud. The cold, clean breath of the winter wind is quiet here. Stillness dominates. Life slumbers, gathering its energy in anticipation of being reborn again.

I think about Dani, Michelle, Greta, and Nicole. All of them, spiraling in my tiny insignificant world, wounded by me. All of them want to love me in their own unique way, and me searching for pure acceptance, unable to receive the gift they are offering—disregarding them as nothing more than reasonable facsimiles of love. The empty vessel of my heart holds no narrow-minded malice for them. I reserve that for myself. Is my soul so full of wanderlust and pererration that it is impotent in the world of love?

The water forms a large pool of clear marsh water along the path—the soft wet soil filled with tall, limp grass, cattails, and sedges. The placid water is lifeless at a distance, but looking closer, I can see that it's coursing with life. Tiny brown schools of fish dance between the small, green, fluffy aquatic plants. Bubbles of air break the surface of the water only to disappear. Life. Clumps of red-eared slider turtles sun themselves on trunks of long-dead trees strewn about the shallow water. Does life ever truly slumber?

At the marsh's edge, I feel the need to meditate. Sitting on a large stone, closing my eyes, I begin. A flurry of unattached thoughts passes rapidly through my mind.

The ocean.

Nicole.

Green tea ice cream.

Clock radios.

Jools Holland.

Nicole.

Brian Eno.

My father.

Sliced American cheese.

"I can't do this."

"Focus!"

"Stop yelling. I can't."

My scattered mind clumsily and repeatedly throws itself with abandon into a mental steel plate, ringing it like a gong with each attempt. Every loose thought effortlessly passes through the blockade like an apparition walking through walls, but my attempts to find nothing bear no fruit. I hate this.

Before, in what seems like another life, I could sit with my eyes closed for hours and in nothingness at the click of someone's fingers. I've lost the plot. I'm severely rudderless and no more complex than the simple protozoa swimming in this marsh. Disgusted with myself and another failed attempt, I open my eyes to see a great blue heron a few yards in front of me. He's standing still as if cut from marble in six inches of marsh water. He's watching me. I stare back, focusing on the ink-black pupil that dots his perfectly round, curry-colored eye. Letting the impromptu staring competition come to me. A profound calm overtakes me the longer I gaze into the empty black space of his retina. What can my life be compared to when I consider the dewdrop shaken from the heron's bill that reflects the full light of the sun? Like that drop of water, light and love should pass through me, but I remain uneasy with that responsibility. Seconds turn to minutes. I slowly feel a slight sensation of peace. Without warning, his long neck flexes, sending his bill with engineered precision cutting through the motionless water below to snare an unsuspecting fish. Success! In that fragile, delicate moment, we are both momentarily made full.

CHAPTER 8

On my way to Asha's for dinner, I stop by a grocery store to pick up a small gift for the occasion. I was raised never to show up empty-handed to someone's home. Standing among the plants and flowers, I'm having a difficult time choosing what to get. It needs to be something unromantic and straightforward. Flowers? No, that seems too personal, like this is a date. Balloons? You're not going to a five-year-old's birthday party. How about a cactus? Nothing says this isn't romantic more than a prickly cactus. This is all too much. A small, unassuming leathery-skinned snake plant checks one big box on my list. No romantic overtones. Sold.

Pulling into Asha's driveway, my phone rattles with a text from Greta.

"So, am I going to see you tonight?"

"Probably not. I've been busy, there's a water leak in my place, and I've been staying in a crappy hotel room. I haven't slept well for days. I'm totally exhausted."

She quickly replies, "Would you buy any of that crap if I said it to you?"

Taken aback and not in the mood for her accusatory tone, I am not in a place to be toyed with anymore. I gave Dani her walking papers this morning and am not afraid to do the same to Greta. I type, "I'm sorry that you feel..." and instantly delete it. I'm NOT sorry. I honestly don't care about your feelings when you care so little for mine. You constantly push me when I don't want to be. It's always about what you want. Do you ever consider me? Earnest proclamations that are not meant for Greta alone. I pause, hoping to let my harsh malice for the situation subside before sending my reply. It's no use; it's time to clean the slate.

"I'm not selling anything for you to 'buy.' If you refuse to hear my truth, then simply stop texting me," I fire off haphazardly, entirely on purpose. Ending with, "Sorry, this isn't working for me." With nothing more to say and no reply expected, I toss my phone on the passenger seat. Calmly muttering to myself, "Well, that's two down."

I knock on the front door, the sound of clicking locks, and the door is open, revealing Asha dressed in a t-shirt and jeans.

"Good evening," she says.

"Good evening, here's a little thank you for the dinner invitation," I reply, handing her the plant.

"How wonderful and entirely unnecessary," she gushes as she takes it from me. "It's so beautiful."

"It's an air cleaner plant and very low maintenance," I

say with confidence as if trying to sell it like an appliance and nothing more.

"I shall have to find it a name."

"Yes," I say while struggling to remove my loafers.

"Oh my, excuse my poor manners. Let me fetch your chappals and a chair!" Before I can say no, she's shuffles off to find chappals and a chair.

By the time she returns with flip-flops and a chair, my loafers are off, and I'm standing barefoot on the cold tile floors of the foyer. I slip on the chappals and think about how silly I look wearing these with my dark denim jeans and blue plaid button-up shirt. It's rare for me to be wearing anything other than sweatpants and a t-shirt. So, it's nice to wear more fitted clothes with zippers and buttons for a change—you've got to maintain those fine motor skills.

"Are you hungry?" she probes.

"Sure."

"Splendid. Tonight, I prepared some traditional Nepali food fit for a yogi like yourself. Potatoes with peas, white rice, chickpea tarkari, wholewheat roti, and some home-made yogurt for dessert. I forgot to ask you about your diet, so I hope that this is alright."

"Sounds wonderful."

"Splendid. Please, by all means, take a seat," Asha says, pointing to a large glass and wood dining room table. "If it's alright, please excuse me to the kitchen while I finish my preparations."

I nod while walking towards the table. I stop to notice small pieces of framed art hanging on the walls—orange-brown figures holding pots over their heads in a primitive Mesoamerican style on thick textured paper. I am intrigued by the simplicity of the design.

"What can you tell me about these pieces of art?"

"Oh, those," she peers from the kitchen, "those are nothing special. Just things I've collected on my journey."

"Very interesting. I like them."

The dining room is dimly lit and almost void of creature comforts. I take a seat at the dining room table in a high-back chair. The table, made from a reclaimed door of sorts, is covered in ornate trinkets and crude hand carvings in the wood, all topped with a thick sheet of glass. Black and white checker placemats and simple flatware mark out a table set for two.

Asha appears from the kitchen, "Here are the potatoes," she says, placing a large white bowl filled with large chunks of potatoes and green peas coated with a brown seasoning on the table.

"Smells fantastic," as a thick whiff of chat masala enters my noise.

"Let me collect a few more things, and we'll begin shortly."

"Ok. Can I help?"

"Oh, no. Thank you so much, but I believe I can manage."

Her vocabulary's formality strikes me as odd and very old-fashioned for someone I guess to be in her late forties. Maybe she is nervous. 'Some people are just that way,' I suppose as I brush off the thought with the idea that she doesn't get many visitors.

"And here we go," returning from the kitchen with another two large white ceramic bowls, one heaped with steamed white rice and the other packed with cooked red-colored chickpeas, "please begin. Help yourself while I collect the last few things."

"This looks wonderful. I'll wait for you."

Back and forth from the kitchen, she goes, refusing my assistance with each journey. After countless trips, the glass table is covered with so many dishes filled with food that I can no longer see the door below. It must have taken her all day to prepare this much food.

"My dear, I almost forgot the pulse. How silly of me," she says before half jogging back to the kitchen, most likely not for the last time. Appearing again with two dark navy-colored bowls filled to the edges with a thin yellow boiling hot soup.

"I made a pulse to go with your rice. I cannot believe I almost forgot it. The rice would be utterly tasteless without it," she says with an embarrassed, meek smile. "Again, please begin."

"Are you sure we have everything?" I joke.

"Yes, quite sure this time," said with a broad, full-toothed smile. "I'll keep the yogurt in the refrigerator until we're ready."

I take small portions from each bowl and add them to my plate until it appears full. I begin with a big spoonful of soup. It's dull, watery, and uninteresting. She waits, watching for my reaction. I press my lips together tightly and shake my head side to side and add a "Hmmm" for dramatic effect. She's pleased with that. The potatoes and peas cooked nicely, but the masala's heavy-handed coating makes them hard to swallow. I go back to the steamed rice for safety to clean my palate. The chickpeas are nice with the tomatoes, but the masala is overpowering. I'm not a picky eater, but I struggle not to appear ungrateful.

"Your rice seems dry. Do you need more pulse?"

"I'm sorry, I don't understand."

Pointing to my plate, "Your rice is dry. When we see that our guest's rice is dry in Nepal, we become concerned that we have not offered them enough food. You are more than welcome to spoon some pulse on it to make it more flavorful."

"Oh, ok. I'm sorry I didn't know that. The food is quite tasty, and there's so much of it. You must have been cooking all day."

"Thank you so very much. I thoroughly enjoy cooking; it's a meditation of sorts for me. I find meditation comes in many different forms. It is silly of me to say this to you as such an advanced yogi as yourself; you understand this far better than I do."

"Certainly," I agree as I think of my own consistent failure with any form of meditation. "Unfortunately, today, meditation is portrayed as a stereotypical person sitting in a lotus pose with their eyes closed on a sunset beach. That's a TV cliché and a common misconception. I can calm my mind in any location, not just an exotic destination," I say, knowing that it was untrue.

"Exactly! In the past, some of my most meaningful mediations have come to me while peeling potatoes or making yogurt."

"My goal is to help people understand that," I should have said my goal *was,* I think as I continue, "The discipline of yoga is not about looking fit but about being able to sit still longer in meditation." Meditation was a touchy topic for me, and I needed to change the subject. "How long have you been cooking?"

"Well, since I was eight years old."

"Wow."

"Yes, I am the youngest of 12 children. When I was eight, my father fell severely ill and was admitted to the hospital. Like clockwork, my mother would visit him daily to care for him. One day while in the hospital, she fell down a flight of stairs, breaking her right arm in multiple places. So, she, too, was admitted to the hospital. My siblings were doing their studies or working, leaving no one to prepare meals for the family. Me, the tiniest creature, stepped up to the stone and began cooking every meal every day for my brothers and sisters. It was something that needed to be done."

"I can't even remember what I was doing at eight years old, but I'm pretty sure it wasn't cooking for my family. Even though thinking back on it, the food probably would have been better if I had."

She smiles and laughs, "It was just my way of making myself useful."

"Good for you. It's nice to be useful."

"Is that your daughter you come to class with every once in a while?" I ask, changing the subject. "How is she doing?"

"Yes, Ziya. She's staying with her father at the moment," she replies, looking down longingly at her plate.

"Oh, ok. How long will she be there?"

"Just until the end of next week."

"I hope to see her sometime. She seems like a sweet girl."

"Yes, she's very timid. Do you know that she is the reason I took your class for the very first time?"

"Really?"

"Yes, I had no interest in taking a vinyasa class. It seemed all too stylish and for the beautiful people if you know what I mean. Looking at me, you know that I am not one of those types. But Ziya wanted to give it a try. After your class, she came back to tell me what a wonderful teacher you are—very hard and demanding. So, on her recommendation, I made my way to hide in the back of one of your classes."

"Yes, I remember seeing her in class one day and speaking with her. After class, she slinked out, and I figured I'd never see her again. It's funny how things work and that I'm here right now."

"Indeed, the universe is always speaking to us; all we have to do is open up our minds and hear what's being said. Do you know that in native American culture, the symbolism of nature in our lives is a language all its own? When we see an animal, it's the universe's way of speaking to us."

"Yes, I'd heard that before, but I know almost nothing about it. Someone told me that seeing a red-tailed hawk was a sign that your elders were watching over you. I'm not sure if that's true."

"Yes, I believe that is true. I have a book about the meaning of all animals in nature. If you like, I can let you borrow it."

"It's funny that we are talking about this. Today I saw the most beautiful heron while in the woods. We sat and watched each other for the longest time. I wonder what that symbolizes?" I ask with curiosity.

"See how the universe speaks," she says with a smile while pushing away from the table. "Excuse me while I find the book so we can look up the meaning of seeing your Mr. Heron today."

While she is in the other room, I finish the remaining

food on my plate and wash it down with a big gulp of water. I think to myself about what an odd person Asha is, but not in an unkind way, just as an observation. The way she speaks is so formal, proper, and carefully considered. I find myself rising to meet her level of discourse. It is pleasant and a much-needed change to speak maturely with another woman; there are no awkward questions about the state of my penis, uninvited nakedness, or aggressive foreplay with Asha. I shouldn't jinx it. I know all too well that even the most innocent conversations can go from discussions of spirit animals to 'Does my butt look big in these yoga pants?' real quick. The universe tends to speak to me in the crudest of ways sometimes. I need to reconsider the company I keep.

"Here it is," she returns, holding a large, thick softbound book in both hands. "Let's see if we can find your Mr. Heron," she says as she flips pages while quickly scanning the text before pausing and pressing her index finger on the page. "Ah, Mr. Heron, I found you," waiting again to process the meaning of the words before reading them out loud. "The heron represents solitude, introspection, soul-searching, inner reflection, and meditation. A heron moves in the blink of an eye and spears a fish quickly. While the action happens near instantaneously, the wait may be long and very still. The heron teaches the quality of patience—of observing and thinking before we act. Does this mean anything to you?"

I'm dumbfounded. Searching for the words as I look up to the ceiling. "Honestly, it means a whole lot more than I care to admit," I bashfully admit.

"Very interesting. It seems that Mr. Heron had something to say to you today. I hope that you were listening," she gently closes the book and sets it on the table. "Feel free to borrow it. It might do you some good."

"If you don't mind, I'd like to read through it."

"Certainly, take your time with it. There's no rush to return it." Noticing my empty plate, she changes the subject, "Well, it appears that you are finished with the food. Shall we have dessert? I prepared some homemade yogurt in the Nepali style. I hope that this will be to your liking."

"Yes, I love yogurt. I eat it every morning for breakfast, but I've never had any that was homemade. I'm excited."

She collects the bowls and plates from the table, moving back and forth to the kitchen. Almost as if in a game, I repeatedly ask to help, and she continually refuses. With all the dirty dishes gone, she returns with a large, circular ceramic white bowl covered with a clear glass lid. She places it on the table along with two small glass bowls and spoons.

"Just so you are aware, this might be different from other yogurts you may have tried in the past," she offers as almost a pre-excuse as she removes the glass lid.

By the looks of it, she was right: I'd never seen yogurt look like this. It looked more like a soft cheese than the grocery store yogurt I was accustomed to that comes in a plastic container sealed with a thin plastic covering that protects the pure white smooth liquid inside. The top of her yogurt is pitted with little indentions, cracked with pencil-thin lines, dotted with flecks of buttery yellow circles.

"Please, help yourself," handing me a spoon and bowl.

I break the rindy surface with the spoon's edge and dig deeper into the bowl, scooping out a healthy helping which

I drop sloppily into my bowl. The thick interior consistency is like ice cream left on the kitchen counter on a hot summer's day. I bring a tiny bit on my spoon under my nose for a sniff—nothing. It didn't smell like cheese or ice cream. Slipping the spoon between my lips, I find the texture is thick and creamy, sticking to the roof of my mouth before the tartness hits the sides of my tongue like a sledgehammer. It is tangy, tart, and a bit sour with no hint of sweetness like the typical store-bought fare.

I swallow while Asha waits with anxious wide eyes and a tight-lipped half-smile for my critique.

"Wow, that's good. You're right. It is different from other yogurts I've had. The texture is phenomenal."

"Wonderful! I'm so happy that you like it. It's something that I love to make."

"Who taught you how to make it?"

"No one. I've been experimenting for years with different kinds of milk, seeds, and techniques. Not to beat my chest here, but there's quite a science to it."

"I'm impressed," I say while bringing another heaping spoonful to my mouth.

"Well, then I shall make you some for you to take home."

"That's not necessary," I say with the intention that I didn't want to give Asha the wrong impression about our relationship. I always strive to keep a healthy boundary between student and teacher. In a moment of blind stupidity and desperate need of distraction, I probably overstepped that boundary by accepting her dinner invitation. I didn't want to cross any further into the awkward ground by accepting a gift.

"So," changing the subject abruptly to something

unromantic, "what do you make of all this news about the virus?"

"Oh yes, I have been reading a lot about it. It appears to be very serious. Many people all over the world are becoming quite ill and dying from it. It's frightening if you think about it."

"Do you think it will impact us?" I ask as I scratch the bowl's edges with my spoon and collect the last bits of white cream before I lick it clean.

"Yes, it seems almost certain that it will. To what extent I do not know, but I am very concerned."

"That's my fear too. I was supposed to travel abroad in a few weeks, but it appears it's all in limbo until things settle down a bit."

"Where are you traveling to, if you don't mind me asking?"

"I plan to travel to Europe and then to India to study. I need a change of scenery to reconnect with myself," I say while trying not to give too much away.

"My favorite author, Joseph Campbell, said, 'Find a place inside where there's joy, and the joy will burn out the pain.' Maybe the change of scenery is inside of you. Either way, I believe it's better to side with caution and stay put. India will always be there," she says, picking up the bowl of yogurt and offering me some more. "Please have some more."

"No," I say with hungry eyes and wonder to myself, 'Are the scars of my pain that evident and overexposed for everyone to see?'

"I have plenty more, and I know how to make more if needed," Asha offers with a large, proud smile.

"Ok, I'll just have a bit more," I scoop another mound

into my bowl and devour it with hasty delight. "It's hard to know what the future holds, though. It seems like God laughs every time we create a plan."

"Indeed, maybe the virus is the universe's drastic way of asking us to take stock of our lives to appreciate the little things that we take for granted."

I agree as I finish the last of my yogurt and push away from the table.

"Would you care for some tea?"

"Oh, no, thank you. I really need to be going soon. I have a very regimented sleep schedule," I lie as a way to excuse myself. "Sleep is one of the most important activities of the day," I say as if reminding myself.

"I understand. As an experienced yogi like yourself, it is important for you to replenish your energy properly every day."

"Our bodies are vessels of energy. It's important to treat that energy with great care," I say with an almost believable straight face.

"If you don't mind me asking, when I see you in class teaching and performing the asanas with such power and enthusiasm, I often wonder where do you get the energy? How do you replenish yourself?"

Challenging questions to answer. How do I summon the energy not only to teach but to get out of bed these days? The larger question is how with my soul so precisely shattered, splintered into a million tiny shards, is it possible to reassemble enough of these fragments to will myself through another day? I exist on the last fumes of sheer willpower, faking it with a smile while my heart slowly withers inside the vessel of my body.

At a loss for an answer, I reply with a platitude that I

once believed, "I love to teach. Helping and teaching others invigorates and fills me full of energy." I smile while amazing myself with that top-shelf nonsense.

"Interesting."

"I hate to say it, but I need to head home and get to bed. Can I help you clear the table before I go?"

"Certainly not. I had such a wonderful time this evening. Perhaps we can do it again another time?"

"Sure," I say unconvincingly. I push away from the table, collect the book on animals under my arm, and move towards the front door. Asha follows, bringing a chair for me to sit on while exchanging my chappals for my shoes.

"I appreciate you having me over. The food was wonderful, and the yogurt was delicious," I say with a warm smile as I stand to leave.

"You are most welcome. And thank you for the lovely plant. I shall have to find a name for him. It's very presumptuous of me to assume it's a boy," she replies with a laugh. "Perhaps I'll meditate on his name."

I laugh as I unlock the door, say my goodnights, and head outside to my car. A luminous waning moon hangs against the thick clouds of a starless winter night sky. I pause for a second to bask under its rays, feeling strangely refreshed and energized in the experience of the evening. An uneasy feeling arrives in me—maybe, just maybe, everything will be alright after all.

CHAPTER 9

Buzz. Buzz. Buzz. The monotonous sound breaks a rare deep sleep of text messages. I look at my phone. 2:42 AM. It is too late (or early) for texts unless someone has just died. Even then, it's questionable. Someone is dying every second of every day, so there's genuinely no need to text me with that worthless information. I'm alive, and they're dead. Text me at a more reasonable hour.

It's from Dani. I thought we discussed everything that could be discussed, but she had a few parting shots at a quarter of three.

"Before I begin, let me say that I don't hate you. I hate that I love you. I hate the fact that you don't love me. If you love this other woman, then you should tell her. My dead husband NEVER told me he loved me. I am a strong, beautiful woman that deserves to be loved. I deserve someone to love me unconditionally. I want someone to fight for me!"

At least no one was dead, but I think I would have rather received a text about someone dying. I pile up the uncomfortably thin bed pillows against the plastic headboard, pull myself up to a seat, and read Dani's text two more times. It seems more like a hostage demand letter rather than a way of closure. I shake my head with exhaustion, trying to make sense of it.

I understand hate; I get that she hates me, even though she specifically says she doesn't—it's implied. What I don't understand is that she believes she 'deserves' love. As human beings, who are we to demand and proclaim that we deserve love? Merely being alive does not merit us a single thing, not even our next breath, and certainly nothing as stunningly beautiful and momentarily elusive as love. Loves ethereal nature refuses to be forced into submission and made to heel like a dog. Who wants obedient and manipulated love?

I've heard the 'I want someone to fight for me!' line before from Nicole. She said it to me right before we split. I believe she said it to her ex-husband too. It always struck me as a one-sided, cowardly, immature thing to say. "You should fight for me, do what I want, but I'm still kinda on the fence about you."

"I'm fighting for you!"

And then it ends with, "Never mind, can we just be friends?"

My heart flooded and burst with sorrow. Sadness knowing that in all of this self-centered "fighting for me" nonsense, no one was fighting for me. Who fights for the fighters, the forgotten ones used and thrown aside without a second thought? Is my imperfect and blemished soul worth less than yours? Is my truth not worth fighting for too?

So, in keeping with the theme of things not to do at 3 AM, I type out a foolish email to Nicole:

I believed I was required to fix our relationship. As I continue to learn, some problems are not instantly solved.

In the beginning, my fluid organic nature washing against your structured planner of the future was a great attracter for both of us, but in the end, time's tide came for us. The day-to-day life or death struggle with the studio, watching you take on every task while attempting to tame your own future's chaotic uncertainty, created a tremendous amount of anxiety inside of you. It was so difficult to watch you suffer. I wanted to help, but your rigid 'I am independent. I can do this!' nature told me that there was no room for my assistance. All I could do was watch from the sidelines. It was painful for me. You were holding on to everything so tightly that you started to lose yourself along the way.

Our histories shape who we are. My unresolved emotional issues handicapped me, created distrust for you in me. Part of your history shaped doubt for me about you too. I knew your nature was to burn down the world to get what you wanted; over time, it was unsettling—it became like rocket fuel for the slow-burning flame of my cautious nature. My heart was so full of love for you; it blocked my brain from receiving the message of caution my gut was sending.

As my uncertainty about us grew, I felt like I was a means to an end and not a partner on the journey. I pulled away while I tried to sort out how I fit into 'our' future. All the while, I started to believe that there was no 'our future,' just *your* future with me in it.

This reality took hold of my heart, and it finally gave way. My brain received the message. I fumbled to communicate this to you in my own terribly awkward way. I told you these things because I genuinely loved you, wanted to succeed with you, but it was too late, you took it the wrong way... our world began to burn.

The last time we made love told me that things were over—just two people going through the motions moving in different directions simultaneously. Our love-making used to bring us such great pleasure, unbridled intimacy, and pure happiness. I was immensely sad, full of guilt. While grieving the death of us, I slid away.

We held on for a while longer, but only half-heartedly.

I will miss the little moments of our time together, a million tender seconds. I cherish these memories and hope that you will too.

Maybe somehow, some way in this endless universe of things, we'll find each other again. I will always hold a flame for you, hoping that it will light a way for you to discover all the things you want in life.

As I hit send, I went numb. I didn't ask for any of this, or did I? Here, in the silent darkness of this seedy hotel room, I stopped to stare. Is love blind faith or just some sort of technique? Unfortunately, I possess neither. No sensation of peace arrives upon the reexamination of my love. Just a realization that discovering where I don't want to go is as important as realizing where I do want to go. Can I overcome my absent-minded missteps and abject failures in love? My soul has a voracious appetite for love while somehow equally being ill-equipped to handle what I receive. Every sense was employed and screamed for the experience of life as I frustratingly languished in a downward spiral of wasted circular thoughts. Simultaneously, my flaws revolted and utterly fascinated me. Will these banal things define me? In the perpetual emergency of this thing called life, does it even matter anyway?

"Probably not. Koans for another day," I mutter as I roll over, close my eyes, and beg for the tide of sleep to overtake me. Its waves crash on my rocks but never fully reach me.

CHAPTER 10

"Sir, are you in there?"

Knock. Knock. Knock.

"Sir, It's me, the hotel repairman. I'm back to fix your heater. Are you in there?"

"Yes, I'm here," I growl with my face down in a pillow. "Can you come back later?"

"Sorry, sir, I can't. My boss says I need to get this fixed now."

"Hold on." I slide from between the sheets and onto my sore feet, slip on some clothes, and open the door—my God-fearing chubby, short-fingered repairman dressed in his sunglasses, vest, and hat waits.

"Good morning," I say with annoyance.

"Good morning, sir. I have the part to fix your unit. Can I come in?"

"That was fast, but there's really no need. I'll be checking out today. After I'm gone, you can take all the time you need. I'd prefer that you come back."

"Sorry, sir, but I can't put off things for tomorrow that I can get done today."

"You are a persistent fellow, aren't you?" I say with a snicker. "I do admire your dedication. You wait for nothing. What's your name again?"

"Fredrick, sir."

"Nice to meet you, Fredrick. Please come in and do what you need to do."

"Thank you, sir."

Fredrick steps over piles of my dirty clothes and unmade bed as he makes his way to the window heater.

"Your wife not with you today, sir?"

"My wife?" I say, confused and a bit annoyed by his probing questions.

"Yes, sir, that pretty lady in the red dress that was here yesterday morning when I was here. You must have done something awful to make her cry like that."

"Oh, her," I say while emptying spent coffee grounds from the coffeepot into the trash. "That wasn't my wife. She was just a friend."

"She sure was upset." He pulls out his screwdriver and begins removing screws from the worn metal front of the window unit.

"Yes, she was, but she'll be fine, I'm sure."

"You must have broken her heart or done something really bad to make her so upset," he continues his intrusive interrogation.

"Love is consistently inconsistent, my friend. Consistently inconsistent," I admit while filling a plastic cup full of water for coffee in the bathroom sink. "An unrequited love is the most painful of all types of love, Fredrick. It hurts deep down in your bones. You know what I mean?"

"Yes, sir, I hear what you're saying. I know how that feels. I lost everything—my house, my daughter, my job, even my dog. It damn near broke me. All I had left was my beautiful wife," he continues working while he speaks. "Her love carried me through it all." With the panel open, his hands deep inside the unit, now pulling on clumps of dusty red and white cables searching for a connector.

"I'm sorry to hear that," I say with the appearance of wanting to care to hear his tale but with no real intention of listening.

"No need to be sorry, sir. It was the best thing that ever happened to me." His right arm reaches deeper into the belly of the machine, blindly fumbling for something just out of his reach. I couldn't see his eyes because of his dark sunglasses, but the curious expression on his face tells me he is so close to what he was after. Unsuccessful but not fazed in the slightest, he pulls his arm out of the metal beast, his shirt sleeve covered with a thin layer of dust. He grabs another screwdriver and begins removing more screws from the gray metal control panel. I suppose that there's more than one way to fix something.

"The best thing that happened to you, huh?" I ask, keeping the conversation going. How can what appears to be the worst thing that could happen to someone be the "best thing"? I pace my curiosity as I sip on my hot cup of tasteless muddy water. "Why do you say that?"

"I thought I had everything in my life that I could ever want," he says while pulling on the control panel with a slight jerk. It comes free in a cloud of clumpy brown dust and debris. "It took a hurricane to come and take everything away from me to realize that everything I thought I had meant absolutely nothing."

"And your wife helped you realize this how?"

"Women are curious creatures, sir. They can see things in us that we can't see ourselves sometimes. My despair took me to the dead-end of my life. I wanted to give up and die. I even thought about taking my own life. You know the stories of men on death row about to be executed and how they suddenly find God? They are at their lowest. There's no going back for them. They need God's love to pull them out of the pit. I was a broken man, sir. I needed God's love to pull me out. My wife's faith in God and me pulled me through. Every day she prayed and prayed, not for our dead girl but me. I needed to let go of everything so that I could make room for God."

"You don't say?" I had my own exhaustive opinions about God. It makes me uncomfortable to hear someone speak about God and the warm embrace of his love in such a blind, seemingly fool-hearted way.

"Honest to goodness," Fredrick says as the guts of the machine and all its colorful wires, plastic harnesses, and copious amounts of dust are on full display now. "Lemme ask you a question, sir."

"Ok," preparing myself for what I know is coming next.

"Do you believe in God?"

"No," I say plainly with rapid-fire precision to his obvious question.

"Hmmm. I'm sorry to say this, sir, but that makes me sad," he says as he removes connectors from a green circuit board with its transistor and resistors. "I've got to reset the board before I can connect the motor assembly," he explains as if I was taking notes. "You know God still loves you even if you don't believe in him."

"That's nice of him. I need all the help I can get," said with a crooked cocky smile.

"He'll be there when you need him. I've no doubt," he says with utmost confidence. Folding and reassembling the mass of wires, he drops the control panel back into place and begins screwing it down.

"I have my doubts; I always have. I don't mean to sound rude, but I need a God who believes in me because there is no God without me. Don't get me wrong; I was raised in the church. My father was a churchgoer. He made me attend all the services, sing all the songs, drink the cheap communion wine, eat those stale crackers, and kneel in prayer. Always kneeling in prayer. I'm certain that he believed I could find God through those ways of submission, but all I ever got were sore knees. When I asked him questions about God, he couldn't give me any answers other than 'You have to have faith.' Faith. I'm sorry, but it seems like a scam," I feel my blood pressure rise as I speak. Defending my lack of faith to someone of deep faith always annoys me. I feel as if I was being sneered at with trivial pity by these feckless rubes as if my attendance into the open arms of God's lukewarm, snuggly hugfest had not been requested. I want to yell at them, "It's a conman's shell game!" But what's the point? Let them find out in their empty-headed way.

"It's no scam, sir," Fredrick assures me while he places the front metal sheet back in place with screws while he clicks some control knobs.

The heater roars to life like a wild and unruly beast.

Fredrick places his palms a few inches from the vent. I sense his unwavering calm energy. After a few seconds, as if obeying his command, the machine's roar quiets to a purring low rhythmic drone. Still offering his hands forward, he spreads his stubby fingers wide and closes them as he feels the rush of air move between them. The air wafting across the room strikes my face with a warm, brittle slap.

"Sir, I think that should do it," he declares with confidence without looking at me. His hands still facing the vent as if transferring a bit more healing energy before he turns away to pack up his tools.

"Well, Fredrick, I appreciate you getting it fixed so fast. If everything in life could be this easy, right?"

"Nothing in life is easy, sir," Fredrick says with a straight face. "Nothing."

"I second that emotion," I reply with a smile.

"Keep searching for God, sir. He wants to give you his love. He will show you the way past all your hardships."

"What does he want in return?"

"Nothing but..."

I didn't let him finish. I didn't want to hear what he had to say. I interject to ask, "Isn't your omnipotent God nothing more than an insignificant and jealous God that requires you to put no other Gods before him? I don't mean any disrespect, but that's how I see it. How can he be so all-knowing, dreadfully obtuse, and blatantly juvenile at the same time? As Gods go, he seems pretty weak."

"God's love is inside each one of us, sir. You got to believe. Do you believe in anything?"

"No, not really. Well, not any longer at least," I admit.

"What about that?" he asks, pointing to the Buddha on the desk.

"That's different," I say with an arrogant and superior tone as if I was operating on a higher plane than him and his pedestrian work-a-day God.

"Hmmm, is it?"

Annoyed, I begin walking towards the door, "Is there anything else you need to do before you go? I've got a busy day ahead of me."

"No, sir, I believe that's it," he says, collecting his tools before walking to the door. "Be careful out there. God has unleashed a virus on the world to cleanse it of all the sinners. You need to bring God into your heart before his reckoning arrives."

"I'll do my best. Be safe out there." I open the door to let him walk by me into the hallway.

"No need to worry, sir, I have God's love protecting me," Fredrick reassures me.

"I'm sure that you do. Good luck with that."

I nod as I close the door. Again, I find myself completely drained. Why do these conversations take such a toll on me? Maybe Fredrick is right. Perhaps I should dismantle these walls that surround my tiny hardened heart and let God's love inside. What's the worst that could happen? The thought alone makes my eyes, shoulders, and arms feel heavy like shipyard cranes. I'll put that deconstruction off for another day.

I turn off the heater, light a stick of incense, say my appreciation, and fall back into bed. From between the sheets, I wonder about what it is to truly be free. No attachment. No God. I thought I discovered liberation by dismissing God years ago, but somehow, I continue to flounder. Should I also kill the Buddha? Is my dependence on the teaching of nonattachment an attachment that I should sever too? Cutting the strings to all attachments is the only way to enlightenment, isn't it? As I drift back to sleep, I'm ashamed at the selfish thought that murder or death is required for me to live and find my freedom.

I wake up a few hours later. It is time to check out. I toss piles of clothes and shoes into large plastic bags and set them by the door. With care, I dismantle Buddha's alter, wrapping her neatly in a clean hotel hand towel before storing her in my backpack.

As much as I despised this shabby flea-infested hotel room, at least it was my own space. Soon I'd be back in that wretched cave with Mike, among his trashy escorts, and his nonsensical hillbilly-esque wisdom again. As I search the room for any of my remaining hidden belongings, a feeling of sickness swallows me. I dread the thought of going back to that place. "It's only temporary," I tell myself as a way to quell the consuming sickness.

I strap on my backpack with all my things collected, grab the plastic bags, and leave. I take the metal staircase down to the parking lot, past the vending machines sweaty with condensation and rust-covered archaic newspaper boxes, open my car trunk and toss the bags inside. Using great care, I place the backpack in the passenger seat and sit behind the steering wheel. I pause, unsure of where I am heading next.

After a few moments, I jump out of the car and walk towards the vending machines. Through the cracked foggy glass, I scan the contents of the metal box. The flickering neon light inside buzzes and snaps as if transmitting in morse code. I pull a wrinkled 20 dollar bill from my pocket to jam it into the machine. After a few tries, it accepts it. Using the faded keypad, I begin punching in my selections.

A12 Reece's Peanut Butter Cups.

C10 Skittles.

 B2 Potato Chips.

C1 Cheese Crackers.

The machine whirls and springs to life, dropping my selections with immaculate accuracy. I keep making random selections in a frenzy until the contraption tells me that my balance is zero; there's nothing left.

I reach my hands inside, pull the candy bars, pretzels, and lifesavers out. I take my haul back up the stairs and into my unlocked room. I stand by the unmade bed. Slowly, deliberately to not make a mess, I unwrap each item and place them neatly on the sheets. After I finish, I throw the empty wrappers in the wastebasket along with the worthless plastic coffee maker. Grab the desk chair to prop open the room door.

In the hallway, I press my tongue to my teeth and whistle. "Come and get it!" I yell to any hungry rat within earshot. "Everything is impermanent! Make yourself fat and happy before our pitiful little God has his way with you." I scan the hallway for movement. Nothing. "No need to be shy. What's the worst that can happen?" Full of confident anger, I swagger down the filthy hallway corridor strewn with broken chairs and plastic bags full of garbage to the stairs to slowly, effortlessly make my descent.

CHAPTER 11

"Hello, I hope that you are well. I was wondering if we might be able to move our next lesson to tomorrow? If that's not possible, I understand. It's ok to say no."

A text from Asha.

I was back in the familiar soul-sucking surroundings of Mike's recently repaired apartment, sorting through a pile of clothes dumped on the bed, trying to discern what needed cleaning and what didn't. Crisp new sheetrock, door, faux wood floors, and a fresh coat of bleach-white paint went a long way to do nothing more than hide the damage. The air hung still and musty in my nostrils. The toxic scent of cheap latex paint made my head throb.

I pause from my sorting and reply to Asha, "Sure, that'll be fine. What time?" It was pointless; everything needed cleaning. I push the pile of clothes off the bed and into a cheap plastic hamper, setting it by the bedroom door.

"Splendid. How about 6 PM? Would you like to stay for dinner?"

"6 PM works for me. Sorry, but I only have time for the lesson tomorrow. Maybe dinner some other time?" I could sense that lines were drifting out of focus. Best to maintain a healthy distance so as not to give the wrong impression.

"Ok. 6 PM it is. See you then. Have a wonderful evening."

I take the hamper of clothes to the laundry room and dump them in the machine. A few clicks and turns causes the washer to gush cold water into the tub. While the tub fills, I add turquoise blue detergent to the water and watch it foam and bubble. As I close the lid, the machine begins its cleansing gyrations and twisting. "Cleansing requires so much energy and friction," I think as I walk out into the den.

I had the place to myself; I click on the TV to find that every channel is reporting on the virus that is sweeping the world. Millions had already died in central Africa. They were still unsure of how it spreads. Was it via sex or from tainted drinking water? No one knew for sure, but the fear was that it would overtake denser populations like Europe or Asia, where the death toll would skyrocket. It seems surreal, like something out of a Philip K. Dick novel, and almost impossible to impact me. "I really should pay closer attention to world events," I think out loud for no one to hear.

The front door crashes open, bringing a flood of cold winter air, followed by Mike and a well-worn woman.

"Hey man, you're back!" an intoxicated Mike yells. "What do you think of the place?

"Yeah, it looks nice," I reply, annoyed that my solitude is disturbed.

"It's like the Taj Mahal in here, isn't it?"

I am confident he's referring to a strip club of the same name, not India's famous mausoleum. "Yeah, they did a good job getting it cleaned up. It looks good," I say as my eyes leave Mike's and glace to his guest.

"Oh, sorry, Tiffany, this is Ian. Ian, Tiffany," pointing to each of us as he trades introductions.

"Hi," I nod with a closed-lipped smile.

She struggles to find a reply as she flashes a clumsy grin with her eyes half-closed. A mess would be a generous way to describe her. So drunk that she struggles to stand, consistently catching herself on the arm of the sofa to right herself repeatedly. Her body language tells me she is in her mid-30s, but she could easily be confused for being 50. Skin a tobacco brown, hair bleached yellowish blonde straightened, the dark circles under eyes accented by thick mascara coating her eyelashes. Her clothes smell like cheap cigarettes and perfume. "So, this is what misery smells like," I think to myself.

After a few minutes, she finally giggles a drunken "Hi" with a wave of her right hand. Good to know that she's coherent enough to understand basic words. Mike sure knows how to pick them. I look at him and ask with my eyes, "Is she ok?" He replies with an affirmative nod.

"I'm going to make some drinks. Who needs one?" Mike blurts out.

"I do!" Tiffany says with extreme confidence. The same person who struggled with a basic 'hello' a few minutes earlier and the last person who needs another drink.

"Ian, you want one?" Mike asks.

"No thanks, I'm good. I've got a long day of teaching tomorrow."

"Oh, so this is the guy you were telling me about, Mike?" Tiffany says, successfully stringing a sentence together while looking at Mike and pointing to me. "He told me that you do yoga. Hmmm," she purrs like a feral cat in the dying days of its last heat as she looks me up and down like a piece of meat on a skewer. "I used to do yoga, but not anymore. I loved the way it made my body feel. Can you make my body feel like that again?" She drunkenly jerks and gyrates her body to demonstrate.

The lame double entendre is as clever as a pillowcase full of shit-stained diapers and makes me roll my eyes up into my skull. Mike rushes forward with a drink, stuffs it in her hand to bring Tiffany's attention back to him.

"Cheers!" he raises his glass with a fake toothy smile.

"Cheers!" Tiffany replies. Still focused on me, she asks, "You didn't answer my question. Can you make my body feel that good again?"

"Are you asking me if I'll have sex with you? Because if you are, that's one of the most inept, lame, and sexless ways that I've ever been propositioned. By the way, isn't that what Mike is here for?" I question. "I guarantee that he'll give you at least three minutes of that 'feel-good' sensation you desire," I say with snarky annoyance as Mike's face goes pale as the freshly painted walls.

"No, I don't want to have sex with you," looking me straight in the eye. "I want to have sex with both of you at the same time." Her eyes dart back and forth from Mike's eyes to mine, looking for a reaction.

Mike's face beams like an idiot child sitting on Santa Claus' lap, telling him what he wanted for Christmas. "I want a Millenium Falcon. I want a yellow and gold LeBron James basketball. I want a fire engine red carbon fiber dirt bike. Oh yeah, I almost forgot. I want to have three-way sex with my roommate and a trashy hooker that I just met at a bar. I really, really want the last one a whole lot. Can I have that, Santa? My papa says I've been a very good boy this year."

Mike looks at me with big moon-shaped eyes and nods his head as if trying to send the say 'yes' message to my brain. I hate to spit on another man's wish list, but I wasn't having sex with Tiffany even if it meant ending world hunger. My dignity was worth something. Also, I was optimistic that world hunger would sort itself out with or without my help.

"Um, yeah, sorry, but that's not my thing. No offense, I have no interest in seeing either of you naked," said with cocky assurance. Mike's dream dashed in an instant. Tiffany, shocked with irritation, it shows it on her face.

"You don't know what you're missing!" she shoots back.

"No, I'm pretty sure I know what I'm missing, and I'm more than ok with that," I stand up from the couch and walk towards my room. "You kids have fun. I'm off to bed. Goodnight."

"You're an asshole," she hisses as I turn, walk back into my bedroom and softly close the door.

"She's not wrong," I think to myself.

In the studio early this morning to a room full of students. They are gluttons for punishment. The more I berate them, the happier they are. What is wrong with these people? "No! Try again this time, do it correctly. It's like you are not listening to the words that are coming out of my mouth." I'm hard on them because I care, or at least that's what I tell myself.

In between classes, I receive a text from Mike. He's angry about what happened last night. As far as I could tell, Tiffany got her three minutes in Mike's saddle of pleasure and left not long after. I'm not sure why he's upset.

"What you did last night was not cool. That girl was going to fuck us both, and you said no. What's wrong with you?"

"I was unaware that I had to have sex with every woman that you bring home," I reply.

"We could have had so much fun with her, but you had to ruin it. You're still upset about Nicole. My papa said, 'The best way to get over someone is to get under someone.' Let her go, man."

I know his intent is well-meant, but his comments just peppers my frustration; they don't knock me out. They just make me angry. Who was Mike to tell me about how to get over Nicole? I could feel the rage boil inside of me. I couldn't just let her go like pouring water down the sink. I loved her. Having sex with other people would not fill the vacant space inside my heart that I reserved only for her.

Mike continues, "I'm not sure if you need a therapist or an exorcist, but either way, you need to get some help. Let her go, man. She's gone, and she's not coming back." His last salvo sends me over the edge.

"You're telling me to get a therapist?! Says the guy who pays for sex. In case you missed it, there's a virus going around right now. I'd rather not get it from one of your cheap hookers!"

Silence.

Maybe I crossed a line. I put the phone away and walk back into the studio to teach another class.

CHAPTER 12

"Now think about placing your foot here and turning your hips forward to the front of your mat," she nervously attempts to maneuver her body based on my instructions. "Yes, more like that. Stop gripping with your toes and relax them. Does that feel different?" She nods yes.

Asha struggles with instruction. I'm uncertain what makes her nervous. Maybe it's my demanding tone or that I'm a taskmaster when it comes to the details. I try not to give her too many queues at once so she won't shut down or give up.

"Wow, this is very difficult. Obviously, I've been doing it wrong all this time. Proof that you can only get so much information from reading a book," she admits.

"I agree. Reading about it and doing it are two different things. I believe that's true of most things in life. Life must be experienced."

"Indeed."

We work on a few other asanas before the session is over. I assign Asha homework, mainly posture focus and pranayama, which I doubt that she will do. In her defense, no one ever does the work; they just show up sporadically and expect immediate results only to later question why their practice never develops past the most rudimentary stages.

"My mind never calms down. How can I fix that?" my students ask.

"You have to tame your mind through breathwork and meditation. The Buddhist Monk Ajahn Chah said it perfectly, 'The untrained mind is stupid.'" If he's correct, then most minds are stupid, including mine.

"Huh? I just want to get a workout to clear my mind. That's why I do yoga." At this point in the conversation is where I usually give up.

"Would you like a cup of tea?" Asha says as she rolls up her mat.

After a long, thoughtful pause, I accept. "Sure."

"Splendid. I'll start the kettle."

I roll up my mat. Collect my blocks and straps, stuffing them inside my bag. I wander through Asha's den after she moves to the kitchen. It's a large room with high vaulted ceilings, dark rustic wooden beams, and warm brown hardwood floors. A monolithic modern gray leather couch hardly fills the space with all its chrome trim and sharp corners. The fireplace dressed with large tan stonework extends along the back wall, disappearing into the ceiling. A large rustic piece of wood that matches the beams above, fashioned as a mantle, hangs over the fireplace hearth.

Two tiny brass elephants flank a simple but commanding bronze Amitabha Buddha in a seated position holding a dhyana mudra on the mantle. It's known as The Buddha of Immeasurable Light and Life, the bestower of longevity vision of the dharma, community, and true nature united in serene harmony. I pause to offer my respects before noticing that hanging above the Amitabha is a large hand-carved painted wooden mask of Tara, the "star," and the Buddha in the female form. The great protectress, the one who saves through compassion. Oneness with every living thing. My cold, starved, lightless soul tingles with a sensation of reignition. I bow my head to offer a 'thank you' before greedily begging for her protection and, more importantly, her endless compassion. Numb with dismay, I feel unworthy.

"Oh, there you are. The water is ready. What type of tea would you care for? I have many options. Please take your pick," Asha says from the kitchen while holding a wooden box.

"Anything is fine with me. Just nothing caffeinated. Caffeine keeps me up at night lately," turning my head to Asha. I return my attention to Tara, bowing respectfully one last time before pivoting on my heels, walking towards Asha, who hasn't moved.

"Are you a Buddhist?" she asks.

"Yes. Well, I try my best," I bashfully admit.

"Please pick something you like," opening the box like she's presenting me the crown jewels of Monaco. Inside are dozens of tea bags wrapped in gold foil precisely placed in neat rows. I run my fingers along the crisp edges of the wrappers and randomly pull a selection.

"Decaffeinated turmeric."

She takes the bag, box, and turns back to the kitchen, "Please let me get you a cup and some hot water."

"Ok," I follow her.

She stops, turns to look at my bare feet as I'm about to cross onto the red-brown Saltillo tile kitchen floor, "Have you lost your chappals?" She instantly recognizes the embarrassment on my face and quickly apologizes, "Please forgive me; I didn't mean to be rude, especially to my teacher. It's a matter of cleanliness for us here."

"Sorry, I'm not used to wearing flip-flops, I mean chappals, in the house. I live most of my days barefoot. So, it's perfectly natural for me to walk around like this. Let me find them." I walk back to the front room where I had left them and slip them on. Coming down the hall is a sleepy-eyed girl I recognize from the studio. Rubbing her eyes and yawning, she's shocked to see me standing in front of her.

"I think I know you," I say with a warm smile.

"Yeah," she mutters sheepishly. "You teach yoga, right?"

"Correct. I haven't seen you for a while. How have you been?" I offer in a bit over-friendly matter to counteract her teenage meekness.

"I'm good. Busy with school. Yeah, I don't come to your classes because they are too hard for me. I feel so weak in your class," she says with an honest smile and an innocent head tilting shrug.

"Nonsense."

"Oh, Ziya, you're awake. You remember Mr. Ian from the studio, yes?" Asha says from the doorway.

"Yes, Mom. I remember him. How could I forget? I was sore for a week after taking one of his classes."

I smile. Ziya is a little nervous creature like her mother with a dark complexion and long, pitch-black frizzy hair, which she keeps pulled back in a loose ponytail. Perpetually looking down with her shoulders rolled forward, you can sense her teenage energy subdued in a cage of insecurity. Occasionally and only for an instant will she flash an enormous smile where her pure white teeth contrast against her brown skin.

"Ziya, would you like some tea? I'm making some for Mr. Ian," Asha says from the kitchen while pouring hot water in a dark blue teacup decorated with painted white cherry blossoms.

"No thanks, Mom," she says as she wanders into the kitchen, opening the freezer to remove a bag of frozen fruit. "I just want a bowl of fruit."

"Suit yourself," Asha says almost dismissively. "Ian, I believe your tea is ready. Shall we take it on the den sofa?"

"Sure." The annoying tip-tap of my chappals makes a disturbing racket on the hardwoods as I walk towards the den. I take a seat on the massive leather sofa as Asha hands me my cup of tea.

"Thank you," I say as I accept the cup. I feel awkward. The sofa's uncomfortable clinical aesthetic makes me feel like I'm there for an outpatient procedure rather than a casual cup of tea. My awkwardness is compounded when Asha decides to kneel on the floor next to me rather than sit on the sofa. I hope she won't ask to kiss my feet again.

"Ok, well, it was good seeing you again. I'm off to study," Ziya announces with a wave from the den doorway with a white ceramic bowl filled with frozen fruit in her other hand.

"Good to see you again, too," I say with a smile as I

draw the teacup to my mouth for a sip.

Asha and I both fiddle with our cups, aimlessly moving the tea bag around and gently blowing on the boiling water as we search for a topic of discussion. The silence is uniquely refreshing. People spend their lives attempting to fill the voids, the tiny spaces, awkward pauses in their life with meaningless words, sluggish actions, or paltry things to make themselves feel at ease. Contrary to popular belief, silence is difficult, but it can be fulfilling and rewarding if we allow it to be.

"So, can you tell me about how you found yoga in your life?" Right on cue, Asha breaks that perfect, fragile silence.

"Well," I tilt my head toward the ceiling while holding my cup between my hands as I peel away the memories to take me back to the pivotal time in my life, "that happened a long time ago. I'm not sure I entirely remember it all." I take a deep breath, "I guess it all started with my wife Michelle about 20 years ago. She had read about yoga and all the benefits in a magazine and thought it was something that we could do together as a couple. I liked the idea. She found a studio, if you could call it that. It was an insignificant dark space with carpet on the floors, nothing like the studios you find today that are more like cathedrals than the simple spaces they should be. If I remember correctly, the air was always humid and heavy with clouds of incense." I smile at the thought of that place like a warm, familiar hug from an old, long-forgotten friend. "The vibe was crunchy hippie granola and all-inclusive. Students of all ages, fitness levels sparsely filled the room. No designer yoga outfits, performance yoga mats, or any of that nonsense. Just a group of strangers open to the idea of learning the complete discipline of yoga. It seems like a million years ago now," I laugh as I take another sip of tea.

Asha says probingly, "Does your wife still practice?"

"You mean my ex-wife," I corrected her. Asha responds with a telling smile. "No, she quit not long after we started. I believe she got frustrated with what she thought was her lack of physical ability. I kept going. As an athlete, the physical part of the practice was easy for me. I took to it like a duck does to water. Gabrielle, the teacher, called me 'Gumby' because I was so flexible," I pause for a moment to recall Gabrielle. I miss her gentle, supportive, encouraging nature. Unknowingly, my mind swirled with so many questions at that time. She offered me a glimpse of my possible transformation in the dying days of my spiritual awakening.

"The jewel inside your heart is pure," she would say to me.

I had my doubts.

"Pay attention."

"To what?" I questioned.

"Attention. Attention. Pay attention to everything. Through attention, you will find the purity inside of you that yearns to be free."

"Some of us are not so fortunate as you to be so naturally gifted with flexibility. Is that a gift that you've always possessed?" Asha asks.

"Yes. I'm built like my father. He was wiry and lithe but strong as an anaconda. If he got a hold of you, there was no getting away."

"I see. If I may ask, why did you become a teacher? Is it something that you always wanted to do? My apologies, please excuse me if I'm being too forward," she says with a downward gaze and full smile.

Waving my hand and smiling as if it were nothing, "No, I never thought about or had the smallest desire to be a teacher until Gabrielle mentioned it to me. At that point, I'd been practicing with her for ten years. So, I was quite shocked that she told me to become a teacher. I suppose she saw something in me I didn't know existed inside of me."

"That's the sign of a gifted teacher, isn't it? To see something in someone else," Asha interjects.

"Yes, I agree. For me, it's more than just seeing that 'something' in someone else. It's about the opportunity to help cultivate that *something* inside that *someone* that truly matters. But you don't have to be a teacher to do that either, right?" I answer my own question.

I wonder what Gabrielle would make of my severe and sometimes domineering teaching style. I held firm to her belief that intense yogis, through consistent practice, can make real progress in the discipline of yoga. Would she believe that my intensity outpaced the value of my teachings? Yes, she probably would. In my defense, the world of yoga had changed. I'm sure that her style would not be genuinely accepted now. Just off-handily dismissed as watered-down spiritualism in this culture of unbridled, self-important, "look at me" materialism.

Once so keen and attuned to my students, my intuitive nature was now offline, no longer transmitting on the same frequencies. I lost my grip on the discipline. It was muddled with senseless anger, trivial attachments, and negativity. Without a sure-handed grip, I was nothing more than a caricature of a teacher going through the motions—for whose sake I just did not know. I longed for Gabrielle's grounding words of wisdom.

"Hello again, Ziya. Are you done with your studies so soon?" Asha asks in a motherly tone.

Ziya is back in the doorway, this time with an empty bowl. "No, I'm just taking a break," she says with a shy twist to her body. "I just came to get some more fruit. Would you like some, Ian?"

"No, no, thank you. I'm just finishing my tea. I probably should get going soon," looking at my watch for a more dramatic effect.

"Please don't rush out. I enjoy hearing your stories. Can I get you some more hot water?" Asha says in an almost desperate attempt to make me stay.

"Sure." She takes my cup, heading past Ziya and to the kitchen. With my chappals firmly on, I stand and follow her.

Ziya turns to Asha, "So mom, Charlotte's mom said that this virus that's spreading around is pretty dangerous and that we should all be careful. She's a nurse, you know."

"Yes, that's what the news is saying," Asha replies while pouring water into my empty cup. She turns to me with the full cup to ask, "What do you think of all this virus talk, Mr. Ian?"

"Well, if I'm honest, I haven't been watching the news that closely. I've seen reports that many people are getting sick and dying but don't know much more about it than that. I guess it could become pretty serious, but there's so much that's unknown about it," I say with no believability.

"Do you not watch the news?" Ziya asks with a sense of shock.

"No, I have a lot going on in my life. World events aren't at the top of my list of things to care about," I say with a shrug.

"I can't believe that you don't watch the news. I bet you aren't even on social media?" Ziya continues her questioning. I was a bit surprised and embarrassed that a teenager so connected to current events could scold me for being so disconnected. The way I figured it was that the world was going to keep spinning with all the greedy people clinging to it for dear life, with or without my input. I had no control over the world, so why whittle away my time considering things that are not worth it. The idea that we have control over anything is not an illusion; it's just a stupid little trick that we continue to play on ourselves.

"Ziya, leave him be," Asha comes to my defense without my asking. "Mr. Ian is a yogi. He doesn't worry himself with the trivial day-to-day postings on social media or the news's sensationalism. He has dedicated his life to a higher calling of yoga. Isn't that right, Mr. Ian?"

'You wish,' the voice inside my head mockingly barks at me. Years before, I had dedicated my life to the discipline of yoga, but now I had lost my way. With Nicole in my life, love appeared. It came along to recklessly slew foot me, bringing me and my delicate world onto its back. My attachment to her, the idea of external love, seemingly undid all my good work. My "higher calling," as Asha put it, had devolved, making me into nothing more than a dull-witted personal trainer. I miss that connection with myself.

"I try my best," I say with a casual smile. "If the virus finds me, what can I do to stop it? It's beyond my control. We all die, right?"

Asha agrees, "That's a very Buddhist way of thinking about it."

"Mom, that's not the point! We could all die. Don't you want to be safe?" Ziya waves her arms and shrugs her shoulders in frustrated confusion.

"Ziya, it's something to be concerned about, but there's no need to shout in front of our guest. Please be respectful," Asha says very diplomatically and looks at me with an apologetic grin.

"I think it's great that someone so young can be so interested in current affairs. I know that at Ziya's age, I didn't care one single bit about what was going on in the outside world," I say while sipping on my tea. Thinking after all these years, nothing about that had changed. I look at my watch again. "I really should get going," I say with a fake smile as I set the teacup on the counter, grabbing my bag, and heading to the front door. I remove my chappals and slip on my shoes. Asha stands in front of me with a sad face.

"I'm sorry that you have to leave so soon. Thank you for the informative lesson. I'll do my best to practice all the asanas and pranayama we discussed today."

With my shoes on and bag in hand, I turn to the door, "Yes, the only way to improve is through consistent practice. You did well today. Keep working; it gets easier."

Without hearing a word I said, she blurts, "Oh my, I almost forgot. Please give me one moment." She turns and hurries back to the kitchen. I hear a refrigerator door open, the rustling of a thick paper bag, and the clicking of glassware. She returns from the kitchen holding a brown paper bag in both hands. "This is for you. Since you enjoyed my yogurt so much, I made a batch just for you. I can't believe I almost forgot to give it to you. Silly me."

"That wasn't necessary," I say with a giant grin taking the bag into my hands. "I really enjoyed your yogurt. Maybe someday you'll teach me how to make it."

"Certainly," her smile beams.

I say my goodnights and move towards my car. As the front door closes behind me, I hear the metallic clicking sound of a half dozen locks being engaged, followed by the clapping of blinds being drawn tight to seal out the light. The petite hens secure the house like a fortress as if readying themselves for an impending siege that will surely never come. Standing in this suburban driveway bathed in the faint flicker of the streetlight, I don't see the ruthless hoards arming the trebuchets and preparing the battering rams to overtake this place. Where is the imminent doom that these two tiny creatures fear so much? Fear is a prison of our own design.

I place the paper bag with the yogurt in the front seat so it won't spill. Start the car. I look at my phone for messages before I pull away to find a few texts and an email reply from Nicole.

You haven't written any of these emails in a conversational manner. They have been full of statements and accusations and assumptions. Not once have you asked me a question. You're just telling me how it is. I am not here to hold you up. I am not "rigid." I do not "burn down the world to get what I want." I did not "lose myself," and if my history created distrust for you, then you never understood what truly happened at the end of marriage which I told you about multiple times. These are extreme assumptions and misunderstandings of the core of my nature and personality, and you have NO FUCKING RIGHT to have said any of it. If you actually don't get that and actually think that's who I am, you never really knew me. Finally, if you send me anymore messages like this do not expect a response.

This is painful to read. Nicole read my message through a distorted lens of anger. Regardless of how eloquent or enduring my words were, that lens only mutates and bends the meaning of things, stripping them of any actual value. There's no reaching her in this state of hostility. My heart is bruised and torn. Disoriented by the moment, I stare blindly at the car console, paralyzed, dizzy with confusion. The light inside me begins to buzz and fade.

"You'll be ok," I tell myself without a shred of confidence. "You can't let this overtake you. You'll be ok."

My phone rattles in my hand with a text from Mike:

"My papa said to never go out of your way for a so-called friend cos you'll always get the short end of the stick. I opened my home to you, and you act all holier than thou judging me by the company I keep. What I do is between me and the Lord almighty. You don't have no say in it. I tried to explain why I invited them over, but you kept cuttin' me off. Maybe it's best for you to move on."

Still staggering from Nicole's rage-filled email, this hit me like a one-two punch to the head and kidneys. I'd known Mike for over 20 years, and he'd never talked to me this way. How can anyone justify paying a woman for sex? "She needed money for groceries, so we made a trade." Is that how he could justify it? I'm sick at the thought of this timeless transaction. I guess all the booze and easy women were taking their toll on his simple country mind. But it solved the mystery; I had gone too far with him. I tried to call, but he wouldn't pick up—another so-called adult in my life, trading in classic passive-aggressive behavior.

"Should I collect my things and go?" I text.

"Since you are the great keeper of the moral high ground, you tell me."

"Understood. I'll pack my things."

With the engine running, the dry heat blowing in my face, I start to breakdown. Weary of the world's toil with no other place to turn, I begin to recoil. Part of me wants to lash out. To say all the hateful things that invade and continually pollute my mind. What's the use? Why wallow in the mud with them, their hate, anger, and rage? "Just let it go." I resist, refuse to let such worthless emotions overtake my mind.

Tap. Tap. Tap. "Are you ok, Mr. Ian?" Asha says as she knocks from the other side of the driver's side window. "You've been out here for quite a long time with the car running. I was becoming worried."

I snap back to this moment. Uncertain of how long I was lost in thought. I rolled down the window to see Asha's worried face. Unable to muster a reply, I just smile.

"Mr. Ian, you don't look well. Is everything all right? Perhaps you'd like to come back inside for some chai? It would do you good."

"Thank you, but I am fine. I just received some bad news. Sorry to make you come out to check on me."

"Nonsense. This is what friends do. Please, I insist that you come inside just for a moment to have some hot chai. Please, it's cold out here," she says with unusual conviction.

"Ok," I submit to her demands. "Should I bring the yogurt in?"

"No, it will be fine. Now please come inside."

Back inside the house, I swap my shoes for chappals. Still a bit punch-drunk, I walk quietly into the den and sit on the couch. I feel the gentle gaze of Tara watching me as Asha moves to the kitchen. I hear the clattering of metal pots and the pouring liquids. Within a few minutes, the potent scent of ginger root, cardamom, and cloves perfume the air. The smell draws me to the kitchen. I pull out a stool to take a seat at the island counter. She moves from the open refrigerator to the stovetop. I watch her meticulously grate fresh ginger root, pass thick white milk through a strainer full of dark green, wrinkled tea leaves into a small silver pot. She gently stirs the milk, watching it closely, being sure not to let it overboil.

"Oh, you are here. I didn't see you sitting there," Asha says with surprise.

"Sorry, I didn't mean to startle you."

Her body still facing the stove, she tilts her head to me with a smile, says, "Nonsense. Sometimes I get lost in the process of cooking. Remember, it's a form of meditation for me. As Joseph Campbell said, 'Your sacred space is where you can find yourself again and again.' This serves as my sacred place."

Still, at a loss for any insightful retort, all I could say was, "Good for you. Where ever it arrives. Where ever it arrives."

Looking back to the milk, she asks, "So tell me, are you ok? You seemed very troubled in the car."

As I look down past my knees to the floor, I feel the tension in my neck and shoulders release. An internal debate begins. Do I want to tell her what is happening, or should I just play it off with a simple platitude? My first inclination is to act as if there's nothing the matter and leave it at that.

"I've had a few rough months," I suddenly and uncontrollably blurt out. My entire body feels released as if a one-ton silverback gorilla just climbed off my back. I look up, Asha still focused on the milk, nods her head slowly in understanding. I continue with a deluge of random thoughts, "I gave up my life to be with a woman that I loved immensely and believed that she loved me the same way. She got angry with me because I refused to give her everything she wanted, so she asked me to leave. With no place else to go, I moved in with someone that I thought was a friend, but he turned out to be an alcoholic with other issues. When I confronted him about it, he kicked me out, leaving me no place to go. For the first time in a very long time, I am alone in an uncertain future." The gravity of that thought grips me, pulls me down. I'm over-whelmed; my body heaves with emotion. "My faith in myself and people has never been so low," I say, attempting to hold back the tears. "I'm angry with myself for being so naive." I want to feel embarrassed; instead, I feel complete relief.

Without a word, Asha clicks off the gas, removes the pot of chai from the stove. She finds two white fluted-shaped porcelain teacups with a faint floral pattern along with matching saucers in an upper cabinet, and with great care, she sets them on the marble counter. She pours the hot chai from the pan into each cup with exacting precision. Taking the saucer and cup in both hands, she turns to me and places it in front of me. She looks at me with a warm smile says, "Have some. It will make you feel better."

On command, I bring the cup to my lips, blow off the heat to take a small sip. The warm creamy texture of the milk combined with the tea soothes while the spicy fresh ginger and black pepper tickle my tongue. A veil of calmness covers me. The heaving in my chest stops, replaced with warmth and compassion. "It must be the chai," I say to myself.

No words are exchanged as we sip on our cups. I think of my path to this place to say those words aloud to a complete stranger. Words and thoughts pressed so deep inside me. I drew the lines on my life's map with thoughts of my father, Michelle, Nicole, Mike, Dani, and countless others connecting each moment in my mind like a film on fast-forward arriving here at this place, this instant in time.

Full stop at the edge of my known world. The next footstep is a step alone into the unknown void, that dark place beset with trepidation, littered with misgivings. Will I be lost here for eternity or discover the edification I so desperately seek? All I know is that there is no turning back now. The only thing that lies ahead is the consistent intricacies and potential beauty of uncertainty. I squint my eyes to peer deeper as if to catch a glimpse of what awaits in the unfamiliar emptiness before me. Useless. No trick of the light can illuminate my path now.

"Mr. Ian, did you hear what I said?" Asha asks softly.

Staring down into an empty cup to see a drying brown circle of chai, I was considering the future and hadn't heard a word she said. "I'm sorry. No. No, I didn't hear what you said. Can you repeat it?"

"I said you are welcome to be our guest here. Just us two little mice live in this big house all by ourselves. I can ready the extra room for you. It's not much but..." she offers with genuine care.

I cut her off, "I appreciate the suggestion, but I couldn't do that. I'll be fine."

"But where will you go?"

"I'm not sure. All my things are at my roommate's place. I suppose I'll have to wait until tomorrow to get them. I'll figure something out."

"It would make me feel better if you stayed here tonight. Take a shower and get some rest to start the day refreshed tomorrow," she says as she collects my cup and saucer to set it to the sink.

"Again, I appreciate the offer, but I can't. You've been too kind already. The chai was delicious. You are right; I do feel better," I reply with a tight-lipped smile and wandering eyes. "I should go. I know you and Ziya need to get some sleep. Sorry for troubling you with my nonsense," I say, looking for an excuse to leave.

She pleads, "Mr. Ian, let's be sensible now. Where will you go? You can't go back to your alcoholic friend now, can you? It's not safe. Something is not right with him. A friend doesn't treat a friend the way he treated you. Stay with us. If you don't, I'll be up half the night worrying about you."

I push my stool away from the counter, stand, say thank you again for the chai and invitation, and move to the front door.

Asha continues, "If you change your mind, you are welcome here anytime. Don't hesitate to come back. No questions asked."

I remove my chappals, take my shoes in my hands, open the front door, and walk barefoot out into the cold winter night.

"Mr. Ian, your shoes. Please. You'll catch a cold," she says from the threshold of the door.

I ignore her warnings as I wander to my car lost in the humilation of it all.

"Remember, like Mr. Joseph Campbell said, 'If you are falling... dive,'" she offers with full-throated encouragement, certain for me to hear while offering the largest of smiles.

I was already in the car with the engine running, backing out of the driveway before I could process her words. My life's graceless descent operated outside the bounds of any law of physics, rapidly free-falling past the point of terminal velocity, hurtling towards the complete annihilation of my fractured soul. It was too late to learn to dive; a belly-flop may have to suffice.

CHAPTER 13

Pain like a thousand Exacto knives piercing my skin from my neck to my hips rattles me from a fitful sleep. The windows of my car are fogged, thick with condensation, warm breath colliding with the cold winter night. Why is sleeping in a car so uncomfortable? I roll off my side to a seat, try to undo the kink in my neck. Under ash-colored clouds, I roll out of the open door into the bitterly frosty morning to stretch my legs and twist my spine. I feel like I slept in a suitcase and probably look like it too. I walk to the edge of the parking lot along the tree line to relieve myself. My body shivers as I watch my breath turn to clouds of white fog in front of me.

"So, this is what the bottom looks like, huh?" the voice of my father mockingly says to me. "Sleeping in your car for close to a week. I can't wait to tell everyone about how proud I am of you." The onslaught of disgust continues, "I raised you better than this. For Christ's sake, you are peeing in the woods like a stray dog. Honestly, a dog has more sense than you."

"I believe it's safe to say that I'm just living in this moment, dad," I mutter with a tone of indifferent arrogance.

"You're sleeping in your car in a state park parking lot! Do I need to explain the definition of 'living' to you? You're one step above being a hobo; you know that, right? You might as well go live in the woods and give up."

"That's not a bad idea. Do you think I can get internet there?" I say flippantly. I was conditioned to receive a back-handed slap from him for this reply; my body physically flinches, bracing for impact from a blow, which never arrives. I smile. Head back to the car to check my phone. It's still dead. I haven't charged it in days. I told the studios I needed some time off days ago. No one is looking for me, anyway.

I take a seat on the curb and sip on a bottle of water, watching the world wake from its peaceful slumber and remembering that I haven't said my 'thank yous' for days. Too lost in my own sufferings to acknowledge the teachings I hold so dear. I am confident that Buddha would forgive my negligence, or would he?

"If attachment is suffering, why are you so attached to suffering? Why are you unable to release the constricting grasp that suffering holds on you?" An internal dialogue that repeatedly undresses me again and again. "Does the constant merry-go-round of suffering I'm riding somehow make me feel more alive?"

The sun burns away the winter morning fog,

beginning to cast triangular shadows on the parking asphalt that move in a circular motion. "That's odd," I say to myself as the consistent motion of the shape seizes my attention as if I were a cat teased by my owner's laser pointer. Transfixed, I watch the shape bend, transform and move over the cracks and potholes with graceful ease. I hear a deafening screech, and the shadow disappears. The piercing cries continue. I follow the sound of the calls up to the open canopy of the treetops. At the top of a leafless tulip poplar, I can see a redtail hawk intensely peering back at me. With a head jerk and an open mouth, another cry released as if speaking directly to me. I watch him with curiosity.

"Are you talking to me?" I ask.

He replies with a short wail.

"I'm sorry, my beautiful friend, I don't understand what you're saying."

A long screech.

"So, tell me about your day. What's your schedule like today? Are you going to kill some mice and then work out later?" I say flippantly with a big joking smile.

SCREECH. SCREECH. SCREECH. The shrieks are loud, more intense now. He's not here to trade in dull-witted, idle chatter. The news he is impatiently delivering is imperative, but I am too obtuse to translate the message he's transmitting. Dismissively I turn away, returning to my thoughts on my weakness for attachment, consider his appearance as nothing more than an amusing coincidence.

Frustrated with my ignorance, he leaves the safety of his perch, floats to the wet pavement in front of me. I'm impressed by his bold persistence. Cocking his head, he spreads his regal wings wide, elegantly dancing side-to-side on coal-black talons. No fear comes to me. It's as if I'm speaking with an old friend.

SCREECH. SCREECH. SCREECH.

Even with my undivided attention, I can't decipher his message. "What are you saying?" I'm desperate to know.

His dance lasts a few more minutes before he eventually stops. With a powerful, swift flap of his extended wings, he lunges towards me. Our gazes join. His earthy amber eyes lock with my sky-blue orbs. I feel a cold refreshing rush of air across my face as he pulses his mighty wings to soar vertically a few feet from my face. I follow his rise towards the sun through a break in the wispy clouds. He catches a gust of air beneath the sail of his wings. He floats and circles again like a sentry on patrol. I'm secure under his watchful eye.

CHAPTER 14

I pack my things in well-worn cardboard boxes that smell like wet paper. Neat piles of European cut wool suits, silk ties, and polished leather dress shoes separated into shiny black plastic bags for donation. Dying plants are discarded in overstuffed trash bags along with countless other minute personal belongings. I sort through a stack of cards from students with thoughtfully written messages:

"Thank you for being a brilliant teacher!"

"Your teachings changed my life."

"Because of you, I am transformed."

All of them carelessly dropped into the bag. The meaningful, as well as the insignificant trappings of life, slowly shed one by one onto the trash heap of history.

"Is my life becoming smaller, more compact, or am I simply vanishing?" I wonder out loud.

Like a drone ant, I beat a constant path from my bedroom to the trunk of my car, moving boxes and bags of life's meaningless things. The room is empty and the car full. One last time, I walk around the room to say goodbye to the cave I hated with all my being. I find a slip of paper and scribble the words, "Mike, Thanks for everything. Your generosity was greatly appreciated. Be well. Ian." I hold the paper in my hand, reading it a few times before finally wadding it up and throwing it in the trash with all the other unimportant things.

With the heavy bag of life's trash in one hand and the key in the other, I slip out the front door and lock it. Sliding the key under the mat, I turn to watch the sunlight move through the trees as they stand tall on the slope below. In the distance, I hear the familiar crack of a golf club striking a ball. Followed by, as if right on cue, "Fore!"

I won't miss this place.

I'm standing in a humid hallway on the top floor of a Trudee's Self-storage. I pause before unlocking unit 242. Nothing but a thin corrugated metal door is standing between me and a lifetime of more painful memories. I'm surprised that such poorly constructed walls can hold back the stories of my past. Inside awaits all my histories packed away into tiny boxes scrawled with vague handwritten labels that offer the faintest clue to what's inside: "pictures," "books," "art." I am terrified of what demons reside in these boxes. Once released, some of the rawest contents invariably always get left out and never returned to where they retired. Are they ever truly retired? I feel as if I am continuously excavating and burying the ruins of my life over and over again. Some things are better left unearthed.

With my eyes closed, I inhale deeply, click the padlock on the door. It squeaks open. I slowly open my eyes to the dark space to see shapes of furniture, rugs, boxes, guitars, pottery. A lifetime of life's possessions condensed into an 8 x 10 metal shed. I feel worthless. I toss two black garbage bags of clothes indiscriminatingly into the black hole of my life. They crash and bang against the concrete floor like a fat lady falling down a flight of stairs. As if closing an airlock on Discovery One, I slam the door shut and quickly click the lock.

"That was fast. No demons escaped this time," I assure myself.

HAL9000 would vehemently disagree in monotone.

In the self-storage parking lot, I plug my phone into the charger and snap it on. After almost a week of being off, it buzzes uncontrollably with life. A string of messages from Asha arrive.

"Mr. Ian, I'm just checking on you. Please send a reply."

"Hello, Mr. Ian, I haven't heard from you. Beginning to become worried. Are you ok?"

"I'm certain you are well. I would like to schedule our next lesson. Please let me know when is a good time for you."

"I am quite worried now. You know, silence is not always golden. I have made you a batch of yogurt."

"Beyond worried now. I contacted the studio, and they said you hadn't been there in over a week. I considered calling the police. Please respond."

"The virus is making several people sick. I'd like to know that you are healthy and safe. My phone is always on waiting for your answer."

I slouch in my seat, blush with embarrassment that someone is worried about me and my safety. I wonder if Nicole ever thinks or worries about me. Probably not. It's easier for her to hate me. Hate is an easy emotion to access. It's dismissive, visceral, primal, requires no restraint to wield. In an unguarded moment, it can eviscerate and lay waste to everything in its path. Compassion, on the other hand, requires constant, patient vigilance to cultivate. It discovers the elusive balance of diamond eyes, butterfly gentleness, a Herculean heart, and a jaw made of the most rigid steel.

"I know I shouldn't be texting you, but I want you to know that I miss you. I'm not trying to get back together. I know it may be a fool's errand on my part, but all I'm looking for is healthy closure. Sorry if I hurt you or let you down. Unfortunately, our timing was off. See you in the next life where hopefully there we'll get it right," with regrettable impulsive mindlessness, I text Nicole.

What was I thinking? It's too late; it's done. No one can ever accuse me of not speaking from the heart. After everything, what's the worst that can happen?

"Hello Asha, sorry. I was in the woods trying to find myself. I am well. I saw a beautiful hawk the other day. I wonder what the book will say about that. I hope that you and Ziya are ok. Be well." It is a simple text that doesn't give too much away, but one that should keep her satiated for a while.

A few minutes later, Asha's reply arrives, "Thank goodness. You are ok. I've been so very worried about you. If you don't mind me asking, where are you staying?"

"Sorry to make you worry. I've been on a search." I quickly reply.

"I understand. Are you staying in a safe place?" I sense her concern.

"I'm embarrassed to say it, but I'm sleeping in my car in the Pink Bluffs state park parking lot." My mood sinks to a new all-time low.

"Mr. Ian, this is entirely unacceptable! You must come to stay with us. I will clear out the guest room for you. It's nothing grand, but I know a true yogi like yourself doesn't require much. I implore you!"

Pride overtakes me, and I'm inclined to refuse her invitation offhandedly. Am I nothing more than a common beggar? I refuse to take handouts from an absolute stranger. I don't require anyone's help; I'll get through this all on my own.

"You never listened to me! If you did, you would get the fucking closure you need. You send me this whiny text. I'm over it. You told me that you didn't want to live with me or have my kids. I don't owe you a fucking thing. Don't ever text me again. Fuck you and fuck that."

Unexpectedly Nicole's text arrives like a kick to the teeth. It doesn't hurt; It just makes me angry. I push down the emotion, but it swells inside of me. I feel my blood thicken and course through my expanding veins. I'm a man at the bottom, pushed beyond his limits.

Kicked one too many times, I lash out, "Ah, there's the closure I was seeking. It seems that I made the right choice not wasting my life with you. I have only ever spoken to you from a place of genuine care and love. You behave like nothing more than an emotionally immature brat. The world does not heel to your command. It's ironic that you sell mindfulness for a living but possess none yourself."

Sending those words, I want to feel absolved, liberated,

but instead, I'm bathed in the tepid lather of anger.

In the orange glow of the setting sun across the vacant parking lot, the blue and white neon of the "Trudee's Self Storage" sign flickers and struggles to illuminate itself. It purrs, flutters only to abruptly stop again as if in a life or death brawl, like a dying star. In what seems to be its last rush and push, the words Trudee's and Storage blink, fade, and turn dark. All that remains is SELF.

It shines bright with arrogance as the sun humbly resigns itself to the darkness of night. Does darkness surround the light, or does light illuminate the dark? Is dark the opposite of light or just the absence of it? Fear is just a shadow in the darkness, and I stopped to stare for far too long. I refuse to be stranded there. Only with an attentive eye does the light expand and never surrender. Self can never surrender to the dark.

With only my depleted soul successfully stripped bare in that desolate lot, I decide to face myself. I can no longer drown under waves of emotions, hide under dirty plastic sheets, or sleep my life away in filthy car parks. I realize at this moment in time that I must, with whatever desperate effort remains inside of me, drag myself from this desolate place to continue my journey to seek and speak the truth regardless of the potentially painful outcome. With only a thimble of courage, I attempt to wash down a mountain of egotism that's stuck in my throat.

I text Asha, "Ok, I accept your invitation."

"Wonderful news. I will make your room ready."

Life goes on; desperately.

Into the fray, I stumble.

CHAPTER 15

Asleep on my side with a thin line of drool hanging from my lower lip. My eyes blink open, and I feel refreshed as if I'd been in a coma for a decade. I roll over to watch the blades of the ceiling fan slowly sweep by like the hands of a clock. It's 5 AM, and thoughts of Nicole invade my mind. I push away the sheets. Look at Buddha with a smile. Her makeshift altar is a slotted pinewood outdoor table painted pale pea green. I'm happy to see her face as I stand to say my morning appreciations in silence.

Dressed, I leave my room's modest accommodations and close the door behind me so no one will see my unmade bed. In the den, I yawn, wipe the sleep from my eyes as I unroll my yoga mat, and begin my Surya Namaskar. Like the familiar embrace of an old friend, the connection is instant; I'm lost in the movement and breath. After completing ten rounds, I take a seat on my now warm mat, put in my earbuds, click on Eno's '1/1,' and begin to meditate.

I'm only in a calm nothingness for a short time, but it's like meditating in dog years compared to what I could accomplish just weeks prior. My eyes closed, I hear the shuffle of feet across the hardwood floors, the rubbery slap of an unrolling mat followed by intensely concentrated breathing. I open my eyes to find Asha on her mat seated in Ardha Padmasana with eyes closed tightly. Her straight black hair, unruly as if a cattle prod had touched her, is in direct contrast to the blissful calm on her face.

So as not to disturb her, I leave my mat unrolled, quietly tiptoe to the kitchen to brew a cup of coffee before slipping on my coat, black wool sock hat, and chappals to head outside. At the back door, I press the buttons on a keypad to disarm the security system. Once disarmed, I open the door to move to the backyard.

The steam from my coffee rises to disappear in the cold late winter morning air as I sit on a dilapidated retaining wall made of rotten railroad ties. Warm yellow rays of the sun break across the roof of the house to kiss my face. I feel nothing. It is a beautiful respite.

I'm safe inside the high barrier that encircles the yard. Each picket in the wood fence is unique. Some slats bulge while others bend and twist. All show their age with a silvery grey sheen. Inside the wall, a large circle of tan, dry, dormant winter grass waits eagerly for Spring's command to arrive to set it free. Past where the sleeping grass ends, barren, exposed dry red clay and small ivory-colored rocks mingle with shallow roots from the nearby lush green Cypress trees that overtake the landscape.

A murder of purplish-black crows bickeringly squawk at each other as they land in the high tree branches that extend from the neighboring property. Shading my face to block out the increasing power of the sun, I can see them in the trees robotically swaying and cawing to each other. Panic reaches them, making their calls' frequency and intensity amplify to a deafening fervor pitch, as if predicting an impending danger. In the shadow of the cypress trees, below the twisted end of a picket cut too short, slides a gaunt white feline with a marbling of tan and grey spots on her furry back. The warning sirens from above quickly cease. Indigo, as I call her, a curious little imp who knows no stranger, found me one morning weeks before sipping my morning coffee on this very spot. She plopped down in front of me, inviting me to scratch her upturned belly. How could I resist her, the pushy little flirt with her pure blue, cyan eyes?

"Good morning, my friend," I say with an inviting tone as she saunters in my direction from the shadows.

Now at my feet, she meows a reply before flopping on her back to scratch herself in the short lifeless grass. I rest my coffee on the tie, bend down to pet her with both hands. She leaps up to all fours, hurrying she rubs her arching back on the pant leg of my protruding shin bone again and again. With each forceful pass, the volume of her satisfied purr grows louder. I smile.

"You are happy today, aren't you?" I ask as the orchestra of her purr swells in reply.

The door from the house opens, and a startled Indigo freezes at the sound. Through the open door Asha with her still wild hair, sweaty face, and a refreshed smile, appears. Fearful, Indigo pivots, darts into the safe shadows of the cypresses.

"Good morning. Did you sleep well?" Asha mumbles as if still not entirely out of her meditation.

"Yes, I did. It was a restful sleep. How about you?" I say while looking back to Indigo, hiding deep and out of sight in a small pile of dry leaves.

"Not bad. I heard you moving around quite a bit last night. I was concerned that the room might be too stuffy for you," she says, standing in front of me with her arms folded.

"Hmmm, I don't remember that, but the room is very comfortable. Not stuffy at all."

"Feel free to leave the door open if it makes the room more suitable," she says as she turns her attention to Indigo to say, "Good morning, Mrs. Indigo. Maybe one day you will let me pet you."

Noticing Asha's want to pet Indigo, I say, "I guess Indigo is like all things in life; the more you try to chase her, the more she runs away."

"I agree," she replies. Looking back to me, she comments, "I still find it curious that she appeared at the very same time that you came to stay with us. Did you notice that she's only obedient to you, her Zen Master?"

I scoff, "I'm far from her Zen Master, but it is strange that you've never seen her before. She is such a beautiful creature. I wonder where she came from."

"Yes, I've wondered that too. It appears that the two of you were destined for each other. I will leave you two be," she jokes before turning on her heel in the house's direction. "Don't forget to eat breakfast. I made a fresh batch of yogurt last night while you were asleep. It's in the refrigerator for you when you are ready."

"Thank you."

With Asha back inside, Indigo gingerly exits the shadows moving in my direction again. She resumes her rubbing and purring while I drink my coffee as the sun continues its long ascent into the mirror of the sky.

"Life is different now, isn't it Indigo? There's a rhythm to things that didn't exist before. Don't you agree?" I ask with a faint flicker of hope that she'll reply.

She offers no response as she lays down in a tight circle with her head held high in front of me. Her eyes glisten like blue celestite in the morning sun. She's content just to soak up the warm yellow healing rays. I follow her lead, shut my mouth, close my eyes and stretch out on the wall, letting the light from the star warm my aching bones.

Time slips away. I feel rejuvenated. I open my eyes to see that Indigo disappeared without a sound.

"I'll see you tomorrow morning, beautiful," I whisper, hoping she can hear me.

Grabbing my empty cup, I head back to the house. Hang my coat and hat in the closet. In the kitchen, to find a glass container of fresh yogurt waiting in the refrigerator. I remove the lid to discover a smooth, clean white sheet of yogurt. With a spoon in hand, I'm ready to break the surface, but it seems like a crime to desecrate something so delicately beautiful. "There will be another here tomorrow," I tell myself out loud. Since I first arrived here, there is always a fresh batch waiting for me every morning. I press my spoon, penetrating the surface to scoop out a large mound of cream.

"Good morning again. How's the yogurt today?" Asha appears, hair tamed, fresh from a shower to ask.

"Morning, I was just about to take my first bite," I say

before sliding the mound in my mouth. "Mmmm. Yes, it's good. Just as good, if not better, than the first time I tried it. Well done."

"Splendid," she moves past me to fill up the kettle with water before clicking it on and opens the cabinet to remove a simple fluted teacup and saucer, preparing her morning tea.

"Would you like some coffee? I can make some more." The same questions I ask her every morning. It's become a sort of cat-and-mouse game. I offer, and she refuses.

"Oh no, thank you. Sadly, as I've said before, I get very nervous when I drink coffee," she blushes with her reply.

"I understand," I nod while I continue to eat. "One day, maybe you'll teach me how to make this," pointing with my spoon to the almost empty container of yogurt.

"Yes, perhaps. It's very delicate work, you know," she admits in an attempt to shroud the entire process in mystery. "I read in the news this morning that the virus has killed 30,000 in this country," she changes the subject. "I fear that the virus will kill a lot of people before this is over."

"I agree," as I let the subject of the yogurt go again, "the virus is horrifying. I am very thankful to you and Ziya for letting me stay here. I only planned to stay here for a few nights and then... well, you know the rest." The virus changed everything. There were no more classes for me to teach, private lessons, or places to go. People feared for their lives, so the world collapsed on itself. Life paused; when it did, I found myself stranded here.

The kettle hisses, bubbles, and snaps; Asha takes the kettle, begins to slowly pour boiling water into her cup while holding the string on the teabag. "Nonsense, we are honored to have you here. You were in need, and we have more than enough to offer. We are thankful for you," she says while adding apple cider vinegar to the water. I find the combination odd but don't comment.

"I hope Ziya is ok with me being here. I don't want to impose. I'm sure it's difficult for her to have a stranger living in her house."

"She's fine. When you told me to ask her if it was ok for you to stay here, we spoke. I told her we have plenty to share and need to share what we can when we can. She understood. You now may be here longer than you had originally thought with the virus," she says and smiles while bringing her cup to her lips for a sip.

Shaking my head with a tight-lipped grin, I reply, "I agree. Hopefully, this won't last too long. I'll be out of your hair in no time."

"There is no hurry. You stay here as long as you need to. You can't rush nature; it takes as long as it takes, doesn't it?"

"Correct." She's right. I was beginning to sense that all of nature is a playground for the growth of our souls. Nature lives outside the shackles of time and for a good reason. It provides a place for us to experience the awful aches and triumphant joys of life. If we could bend the timetable of nature by pressing the fast-forward button, we would all skip past the painful episodes to only live life's most enjoyable moments, rendering the good moments utterly devoid of value and meaning.

"Will you be going into your woods today to meditate?"

Ever since I arrived here, I take long daily walks into the forest surrounding the neighborhood where Asha and

Ziya live. Nico said it best.

I've been out walking
I don't do too much talking
These days, these days
These days I seem to think a lot
About the things that I forgot to do
And all the times I had the chance to.

I spend what seems like years wandering through the trees and hills observing nature, always stopping to attempt a meditation session during each journey. The results are often sporadic or "consistently inconsistent," as Fredrick would say. Some moments, nothing more than hellish flashbacks to painful memories, while others are senseless longings for a love that has long passed me by. As my external world drastically changed, so too had my internal one, but only in the seamlessly slightest unit of measure.

In the past, my constant meditative failings would eat at my inner being, decay my heart, and leave me in fits of anger. Now, the tug of war for my thoughts seems less important to me. When I fail, which I almost always do, I shrug off the effort with a "that wasn't the worst" consolation.

"Yes, I'll be back in time to teach yoga before dinner," I tell her. Teaching the tiny creatures, as they call themselves, yoga asanas nightly is my most minor way of showing them my appreciation for taking me in during my most desperate hour.

"Splendid, well, I leave you to it to enjoy the rest of your day. As always, please feel free to eat whatever you can find," she says while taking her tea and leaving the kitchen.

I scrape the corners of the bowl of the last firm bits of yogurt before bringing it to my mouth to slurp off the last bits of whey. Feeling full, I set the dirty bowl in the sink; put my jacket, shoes, and hat back on before heading out the front door towards the woods.

In the wilderness, I am home. Among the broken trees, a forest floor littered with decay and its potential for new life. Here the scratch inside me is unflinchingly visible and unsheltered. Any attempts to hide it are fruitless. I arrive each day to shed my skin, commune with life's ghosts, and learn to speak to myself in a new language. Without knowing, I ask the purity of nature to bear witness to my mutilations and heal my soul.

Today I choose an alternative path, one that is full of large moss-covered rocks, slippery red clay, and steep inclines. The going is more difficult with the cold, wet morning air burning my throat and making my nose run like a leaky faucet. I slip a few times on the wet stones but catch myself with my hands, cutting and bruising my knuckles. After a short climb, I arrive at a small crest where the sun breaks through and can see for hundreds of yards. The world seems infinite here. I wonder about the first time man crossed through this place. Did he stop to notice the endless beauty that lay before him, or was he too preoccupied with the immediate task of just staying alive and not being eaten by a mountain lion that was surely stalking him?

Confident that no lion would eat me, I stop to ponder the beauty before me. I climb the thick trunk of an ancient tree shaped like a hand. Sitting in the palm of this proud giant oak, its five large fingers extend upwards protectively, surrounding me. I can see further past the scattered clumps of sleeping dogwoods over the sliver of a creek that trickles water down the hill's narrow serpentine spine to the river that waits in the distance. Twenty yards away stands the dead remains of a tree like the one I sit on. Its hollow limbs gripped in the heavy chains of thick green vines, slowly overtaking, dismantling, and pulling it back to the Earth. An immense sadness overcomes me.

I think about the two trees; what they had witnessed in their 100 years of existence. Against all odds, they accidentally caught hold of life at the same time. They struggled through periods of drought, pollution, heavy rains, high winds, and more than one inconsiderate dog together. They most likely suffered but somehow kept going through this time, becoming more resilient in the supporting shade of each other's growth. At some point, whether from lightning or disease, a companion in life gave way to die. Leaving the other alone in this beautiful place cursed to watch its partner gradually disintegrate. I cry tears of despair; the nature of time can be so cruel.

Protected inside the healing hand, I fight for stillness but quickly resign my attack. With my eyes shut tight, I gradually give myself to the power and energy of the place. My mind floods with koans.

"Am I like this mighty oak? What is my true nature when I think of this tree?"

"Will I pass through this time of uncertainty and continue to thrive?"

"Will I adapt and grow?"

"Am I doomed to live this life alone?"

"Will I arrive differently on the other side?"

"Yes, I'll be unable to hide the twists, knots, and broken limbs that come with this change. Wear them like a badge of honor."

My heart swells with compassion. Without effort, I connect with that feeling, wrap my arms around it, feel the warmth of its grip. In that caress, I am lifted. Like the wind through the trees, my soul screams to be free, and thoughts of my father, his painful dance with the nature of time, crowd the vacant lot of my mind.

A text from my father. He never texted, or called, for that matter. We hadn't spoken in years. Some things were better left unsaid.

"I'm dying." Simple, direct, devoid of emotion, and a matter of fact—the only way he knew how to communicate.

"I'm certain. No, I'm positive that we are all dying," a fast, cold-hearted reply—harsh, cutting, snarky, and regrettable—the only way I knew how to communicate with him.

"I guess you're right, but I want to see you." His words told me that his end was near.

"It's a little late, isn't it? We haven't spoken in two decades." I childishly jabbed him, seeking retribution while in his current state of attrition.

"No, I hope it's never too late for empathy."

"You mean sympathy, right? If so, that's rich coming from you. Please refresh my memory; when did *you* ever show me sympathy? Because all I remember is broken bones, bruises, and a lifetime of painful memories."

Silence.

I felt sick with pride in saying those words, the same sickness I felt during our last confrontation. Me, fresh out of college, full of vigor and life. We argued. He lunged at me, expecting me to cower and accept the punishment as I'd done a thousand times before. I stood my ground.

Surefooted with a solid and deft right hand, I dropped him to the floor. His eyes filled with terror faster than his nose bled. I leaned over his prone body, my arm cocked, teeth grinding, knuckles white, ready to unleash a lifetime of fury.

Stuck in that moment, I said to myself, "You killed the king. Now, are you going to wear his crown?"

My mind burst with an immense quantity of disgustingly nauseating hubris. I paused in search of compassion, uncoiled my bloodied fist, unclenched my jaw, and turned away forever.

"I'm sorry, son," he said from his back while blood gushed from his broken nose.

Silence.

"Ok, I'll come to see you."

I found him in a hospital bed a few weeks later. His bone-thin body, overrun with plastic tubes and colorful electrical wires, rapidly withering away. Skin whiter than the sheets that surrounded him. Face caved in. His new young wife hovering over him, desperately spraying essential oils in the air as if trying to ward off the cancer that was already rapidly devouring him. His sunken eyes cried, and his body trembled as I walked into the room. He was a hard man. He was a goner, so the doctors said.

I made a joke. It wasn't funny.

We sucked on chocolate milkshakes and talked about sports while the choir of Earth's sirens called his name. We signed our truce, threw our dull and rusty swords aside— they were utterly useless and meaningless now.

"I was a shitty Dad," he flatly admitted without shame.

Who was I to argue? "I guess you did the best you could."

"I found someone that loves me, and I love her. I've never been happier than I am now," he reached to touch my hand as he continued.

I recoiled and struck with wicked venom, "You're dying. What do you know about love?"

"Be happy, son. Be happy," he countered with an unfamiliar gentle tone.

"I don't know if I'm strong enough," something inside of me, a hard man made of clay, gave way as I said those words.

"You're stronger than I ever was," tears formed in the corner of his eyes, fell away to disappear into the fabric of the sheets.

I rolled my eyes to the ceiling attempting to hold back the emotion, "Some bruises never heal. I hated you for so long. But I forgive you." The simplest words quenched my soul. I instantly regretted all that time lost, chained to anger in the barren wasteland of hate.

Bathed in sterile white hospital light, we both cried. "I'm going to beat this," he lied to himself and me.

A few days later, with a trash can full of empty milkshakes, I watched him slip away. Confused and powerlessly entranced by the siren's intoxicating call. He was lost.

He looked at me with quixotic fear to scream, "I don't like you. You scare me!"

"It's me, Dad."

"MOTHER." His last word. Concise without emotion.

It struck me as odd. Such a strange last word to hear him say. In all the years of knowing him, I never heard him speak his mother's name. I knew nothing of her. He ran away from her at 14. She never took the time to find him.

That must have tormented him, twisted his soul in that condition, who knows what thoughts cower with fear in the dark corners of a man's heart. Something deep inside of him wanted release, to be free in that last dying gasp.

"Was he was cursing her one last time?" I asked myself.

"He was running back to her."

Reunited together in the Earth, their histories soon forgotten.

"Don't stay in the woods too long, or you might be lost forever," a text from Asha brings me back.

I slide down the trunk of the old tree. Rest my hand on its coarse bark. Bow my head in silence to say thank you for the lesson and protection. I wander down the slick rocky slope as the sun sets and the temperature falls.

I softly whisper to my ghosts, "I'll see you again tomorrow," leaving them behind as I exit through the forest's tree line back into the real world.

CHAPTER 16

"Think about moving your foot here and extending with your leg like this. Yes, that's it. Beautiful." I made it back just in time to teach my only students—my captive audience.

"I have a question," Ziya says with an innocent smile. "I know this sounds like a dumb question, but when I put my front foot here in Warrior II, what should my back foot be doing?"

"Sure, yes, there are no dumb questions," I assure her with a supportive smile. "Try pushing the outside of your back foot down while lifting the inside of your foot up. Make sense?"

She nervously tries with a big smile to squeeze her foot into the mat with all eyes watching. "Wow, that kind of hurts. I'm not sure I'm ready for that."

"Yes, sure you are. You just need to keep trying. It only gets easier with practice."

"I don't have the strength," she confesses with a shrug.

"You have more strength than you give yourself credit for," I say with a wink. "Asha, how did you do tonight?"

Asha, a little weary from the practice, takes a second to respond. "It was difficult for me. Like Ziya, I need to work on creating strength. I understand it will take time."

"You both are doing wonderful," I admit with another encouraging smile.

"I am going to shower and make dinner. I'll be back in just a moment," Asha says as she rolls up her mat, placing it in a square wicker basket before leaving the den.

"What's for dinner?" I jokingly ask Ziya.

"Don't ask me. I don't know how to cook. You know that my mom does all the cooking in this house."

"How is it possible that you don't know how to cook?" I ask, puzzled.

"No one taught me," she admits with a humble chagrin.

"Would you like to learn?"

"Sure, I guess. Is it hard?"

"Is it hard? Not if you know what you are doing. Do you know how to learn?"

"Yes, I think so," she says, unsure of what I'm asking.

"Well, I know you're smart and know how to learn. If you know how to learn, then you can learn anything. Remember, it only gets easier with practice," I say with a big smile and nod. "What would you like to learn how to cook?"

She turns her head, looking up to the ceiling in thought, "Um, I don't know, can we make eggplant parmesan?"

"Really, out of the things you could wish for, you wish for eggplant parmesan?" I ask with a laugh.

"Yes! Obviously, I don't get out that much," she says with a smile. "Can we make that, though?"

"Certainly, that's easy. I'll teach you how to make that."

"Ok, I can't wait," her smile beams with excitement as she claps her palms together in gentle applause.

We finish rolling up our mats, putting away blocks and straps before she heads to her room, and I move outside into the cold, windy night. A thin curtain of clouds caught in the whisper of the wind race by, filtering the lunar rays of the full moon as they pass. On my back in the dead grass, I watch the never-ending race of clouds that overtake each other, some merging to form a grander one while others break apart and dissolve forever. I'm captivated by the action of it all.

A 'meow' from the shadows announces Indigo's unexpected late-night arrival. She saunters towards me with something in her mouth. I roll over to greet her with a click of my tongue and a pat of the brown grass. With an almost respectful calm, she sits next to me, opens her mouth to drop a small brown lump in front of me. She purrs with pride over her offering.

"What is this, my friend?" I inspect her gift. A small sand brown frog with black spots frozen with fear lays in front of me. "Indigo, I hope you didn't hurt this little fellow!" I chastise her as I place him in my palms to see that he's alive with no notable wounds. The inconvenience of it all just perturbs him.

"Sorry, for Indigo, she's a troublemaker sometimes," I

apologize to the frog as he remains still with his eyes open.

"Indigo, you little devil, where did you find him?" she continues to purr with smugness.

I cradle the frog in my hands, walking past the grass towards a large black boulder that sits on the exposed ground. "You should be safe here," I say as I place him under the shoulder of the rock. I walk back to Indigo to give a few reassuring and thankful pets before heading back to the house.

"You leave that frog alone, Indigo," I warn her from the doorway before walking inside.

Asha is in the kitchen banging pots together in a flurry of activity. The deafening high-pitched whistle of the pressure cooker on the stove joins the chorus of noise.

"Something I can help with?" I offer.

"No, no. I am doing quite well. Just attempting to get everything together for supper," she says a little wearily. "I trust that pulse, rice, and asparagus will be enough for you tonight. A true yogi meal."

"As always, it sounds perfect."

"Are you not tired of eating the same meal every evening? I am concerned that you are not eating enough for your level of activity. Always practicing your asanas and hiking in your woods can deplete your body without proper nutrients. I hope you would let me know if you aren't getting enough food," she says with a curious glance.

"Yes, Asha. Trust me; I am happy to eat the same thing every day. I honestly enjoy the consistency of a routine now. Waking up, practicing, meditating, teaching, eating, and sleeping on a schedule is so helpful," I admit. I smile as I reply.

Over the past few weeks, the ritual of life had created a grounding effect on me. Before coming here, my mind had become like my life—scattered, devoid of any rhythm. Experiencing the same day again and again was calming.

Changing the subject, "Indigo brought me a frog when I was outside earlier."

"Oh my, did she kill it?"

"No, he was alive and well, just in shock. I moved him under that large black stone."

"That creature truly loves you to bring you such a wonderful gift as a manduka. It must be a sign."

"Well, it's funny that you say that; my students used to say I moved like a frog on the yoga mat," I laugh, thinking about it.

"Wonderful! So, you *are* the Manduka! Miss Indigo must have known that. That's why she brought you that as a gift. Maybe you two knew each other in another life?"

"I suppose. Anything is possible," I nod. A wave of melancholy reaches me as I think of Nicole and how we once both believed and talked about the possibility of knowing each other in another life or multiple other lives. I think about how I had waited so long in this life for her to arrive. Now, in such a short time, she was gone. I miss her.

"Ziya, supper is ready," Asha announces like a drill sergeant from the front of the stove.

Ziya arrives with a skip and a hop in the kitchen, fresh with her hair still wet from the shower.

"Mom, what are we having for dinner?" she asks, already knowing the answer.

"Ziya, what a silly question. You already know. White rice, pulse, asparagus with some yogurt for dessert," Asha says impatiently as she moves dishes full of food from the kitchen to the dining room table.

"OK," Ziya mutters with disappointment. "Can we have something different sometimes? I feel like we eat the same thing every night."

"Ziya, enough with your complaining. Mr. Ian is a yogi, and we are eating yogi food for him. There's nothing wrong with this food. Now go set the table."

"Mom, I'm not complaining. I don't mind eating this, but a little variety would be nice. Ian offered to teach me how to make eggplant parmesan. Can we have that one night instead of pulses?" she says imploringly.

Asha glances at me with a suspect smile as if I betrayed her. "Well, if Mr. Ian wants that, then I suppose we can make it."

Ziya dances from foot to foot with happiness, "Can we put extra mozzarella cheese on it? I love cheese."

"Let Mr. Ian answer that question."

All eyes turn to me; some are happy, others disappointed. "Sure. We can make it any way you want." Feeling like I created trouble, I want to change the subject; I ask, "Is it time to eat?"

"Yes."

We find our usual places at the large glass dining table. Ziya takes her seat at the end while Asha and I sit on opposite sides facing each other. Clear glass bowls of white rice are passed around, topped with a yellowy pulse and crisp stalks of green asparagus. Each of us taking a bite before making casual comments like, "This is good," or "The asparagus is rather tasty tonight." We don't mean it. After weeks of eating the same thing, the three of us are thinking about the promise of the cheese-covered eggplant parmesan.

After we finish eating, Asha comes from the kitchen with a container of fresh yogurt. "When does she have time to make all this yogurt?" I say to myself. We pass more bowls around, filled with scoops of fluffy white yogurt. We each take a spoonful to our mouths and nod with satisfaction.

"It's not too tart this evening, is it?" Asha asks coyly.

"No, I think it's nice," I reply believingly. I had become accustomed to the tartness of her yogurt since my first visit and now enjoyed it.

"So, do you think you'll ever teach me how to make it?" I ask teasingly.

With a smile, Asha offers, "No one taught me how to make it. I learned through experimentation. It's a delicate process. Maybe sometime I will show you the way."

"Ok, I understand." What I understood was that making yogurt for Asha was a sacred art form. An expression of her true self. She loved the accolades that Ziya and I gave her about her art. She felt immense pride in her accomplishment. Who was I to deprive her of that?

Recognizing my disappointment, Asha continues, "If I were to give you all the steps in the process, you wouldn't be making your yogurt. You'd be making a version of my yogurt. Is that what you really want? Wouldn't you rather make your version? By giving you all the information at once, I deprive you of the journey to find your version, do I not? Do you not say the same thing to us when you teach us yoga asanas?"

With that, the air in the room changes. We are no longer casually discussing how to make yogurt but something much more significant.

"Well, it's not entirely the same. I'm asking for a recipe while you are discussing dedication to a discipline. The two are not the same," I counter.

"How are they not the same?" she becomes defensive. "Both require the knowledge and understanding of a technique. You tell us that we are not required to sit in Shukasana with our eyes shut to mediate and that meditation can be as long or as short as we desire. So, can I not meditate while peeling potatoes or while watching milk boil?" she says with aggressive curiosity.

"Yes, I admit that we live in modern society and that we are all yogis in this material world. And I understand that we all don't have the luxury of living in a cave to spend our hours meditating until we arrive at higher conscious-ness, concentration, Samadhi, or whatever you'd like to call it. I agree meditation can arrive at any time in many different forms, but is meditation a required component of the yogurt-making process?" I say teasingly.

She's in no teasing mood, "I have no recipe. I perform the process without the help of instruments or tools. I just feel it."

The words 'perform the process' stick with me as if she were performing some sort of ancient Aztec sacrificial bloodletting ceremony at the top of Templo Mayor. "Like life, there's no recipe. You can give me all your yogurt-making knowledge, but you cannot give me your yogurt wisdom. Isn't that what you're saying?" I flatly inquire.

"Correct. If I gave you all the answers, then you would never find the discoveries for yourself," Asha says with a firm sense of conviction. "Failure is a more powerful tool for learning than instant success, is it not?"

"This is getting way too intense for me," Ziya interjects

with a nervous smile. "I'm not sure why the two of you are arguing."

"We're not arguing, just having a candid conversation about spiritual growth. Do you not see that?" Asha replies.

"No, not really. It seems like you are both pretty upset to me."

Softly putting both of my hands on the table, I look at Ziya to say, "We are not upset. We are just passionately discussing something bigger than all of us. Growth is sometimes a painful process." Attempting to ease the tension for Ziya, I offer with a smile, "But all I was really after was more yogurt."

"Ha! You know there's always a fresh batch waiting for you, so there's no need to worry about that," Asha says as she rises from her chair, beginning to collect dirty dishes. Ziya follows her lead, stacking bowls on top of each other before turning to the kitchen.

"Supper was delicious as always," I say, grabbing the few remaining bowls on the table. I place the bowls in the kitchen sink, return to the table to fold the placemats and straighten the chairs. "Can I help clean the dishes?" I ask as I do every night, expecting the same reply.

"No, we can handle it. Please take your rest. I am sure you are tired after teaching us today."

Without putting up a fight, I move to the den to take a seat on the oversized leather couch. I hear the two of them cheerfully chattering in the kitchen as dishes chime and water runs. There's a calmness in the air. I reach for an acoustic guitar that's leaning against the wall—a birthday gift to Ziya from years past that she never learned to play. I strum the strings to find it woefully out of tune. Turning the keys gently, I hear the metal strings stretch as if in agony, finally coming into tune. I run my fingers over the strings again, "That'll do," I say to myself. It's been so long since I held a guitar. My hands are tight, fingertips tender as I finger some chords on the old rusty wires. Within a few minutes, it comes back to me. I begin strumming a few chords in sequence, remembering the melody and lyrics. An outpouring of emotion, a song comes tumbling out as if summoning a demon long been since exorcised.

Good times for a change
See, the luck I've had
Can make a good man
Turn bad
So please, please, please
Let me, let me, let me
Let me get what I want
This time

CHAPTER 17

Another morning arrives; life's routine begins again. I pull myself from the sheets. I transmit my 'thank yous,' perform my sun salutations, attempt to sit in meditation, brew some coffee, stand in the frosty morning air waiting for Indigo's arrival to exchange affections before beginning the same day all over again. Asha finds me sipping on coffee, softly kicking rocks and dirt in the barren section of the yard.

"How are you this morning?" she asks.

Preoccupied with the ground, I respond plainly, "I'm well."

"What's on your mind this morning?" she walks closer, looking at the ground where I am standing. "Is there something the matter?"

"No, nothing the matter. I thought that this might be a

good place to create a garden. Spring will be here soon. If we create and dig the beds now, we'll have time to grow some things."

"What kind of garden are you thinking about?"

"A vegetable garden. We can grow tomatoes, zucchini, peppers. All sorts of stuff."

"Even eggplant, you know, for Ziya's eggplant parmesan," she says with a big smile. "I've never grown a garden of my own." She bends over to inspect a few rocks more carefully and then taps the ground with her fist. "The ground here is very hard here with lots of stones. I don't believe it's hospitable for growing anything."

"Yes, we can grow eggplants," I say with a chuckle. I use my chappal edge to sketch out a few crude lines in the ground to show her where the beds will start and end. "The ground will need to be turned first, and then we'll need to add some compost to make it more fertile for growing. We can create our own Victory Garden of sorts to share with everyone," I suggest.

"Victory Garden? I'm not familiar with that term," she asks and looks at me with a curious frown.

"Victory Gardens were created during World War II in America and other places to boost morale and supplement the food supply. We could all use a little boost to our morale right now, don't you think?"

"Indeed. I'm intrigued. I believe it's a wonderful idea. How do we begin?" Asha asks as she sets the stones down with care before standing and patting her hands together to clean off the dirt.

"I'll get some plants and soil. Do you have yard tools, like a shovel or pick?"

"Yes, I have some tools that the previous owner left

when I purchased the house."

"Perfect. That's all we need."

"Wonderful," she says while crooking her neck to look past me towards the cypress trees. "Your friend is waiting for me to leave so she can see you again. Let me leave you, two lovers, alone," laughing as she moves back to the house. "Don't forget to eat your breakfast. You know where to find your yogurt."

"Thank you."

I kneel, pushing rocks away from the ground with my hands, wondering if I can truly bring life to this desolate patch of soil. Indigo is under my hips, arching her back in a flash as she rubs herself on my leg, leaving a trail of long white hair behind. My fingers under her chin, I scratch, and the symphony of purring begins.

"We're going to grow a garden here. Do you think you can police it to make sure no one steals anything? Just don't kill anything. You have to earn your keep, you know," I softly whisper to her. She continues to purr. "Alright, my dear, it's time for me to go eat my breakfast and stare at my ghosts." I rise, wave goodbye, and wink to her before moving back to the house.

In the refrigerator, as always, a new container of yogurt awaits. I devour it with greedy haste before rinsing and setting the bowl in the sink. Shoes and long sleeve shirt on, I head back into the morning air, like a pilgrim journeying to my holy place, to my woods to face myself again.

CHAPTER 18

I open the front door to find Asha fussing with a cardboard box of plants.

"What do you have there?" I say, closing the door, slipping on my chappals before walking over to see what's in the box.

"Well, I liked your Victory Garden idea so much that I decided to buy some plants today while you were in your woods," a look of pride plastered on her face. "I got some basil, tomatoes, peppers, and eggplant," more pride swells inside her.

"Not to deflate you, but it's still too cold outside to plant those right now. We'll have to keep them inside for a few more weeks before we put them in the ground," I put my hand on Asha's shoulder and pat it tenderly as I console her.

"How foolish of me to buy them so quickly. I was so excited by the idea that I rushed out to get these," she offers with defeat before taking the box of plants to the garage.

"It's not a big deal. Where are you taking them?"

"To the garage," upset with herself.

Walking towards her, I take the box, "You can't put them in the garage. They'll die there with no light. Let's keep them in the house. They'll be fine until the weather warms."

A juvenile smile appears as she lets me take the box, "Ok, you are right."

I move the box to a warm and sunny room just off the kitchen and set it on the floor. "They'll be fine here."

Asha agrees as she nods her head. Moving to the kitchen, she washes her hands under a stream of warm water. "How were your woods today?" she asks.

"Wonderful. The weather is changing. New life is emerging. Spring is almost here. Some days I want to stay there forever. The peace that arrives in me when I'm there grabs hold and overtakes me with unforgettable satisfaction. I know that I can't stay there forever, but I want to build and maintain that calm inside me for as long as possible. I feel myself searching."

"What are you searching for?"

"I'm not sure," I admit with a tone of sadness.

"A purpose, maybe? We all have one. Some of us just don't know what it is yet," she replies while drying her hands with a towel, removing a metal bowl from the upper cabinet, filling it with cold water and lentils.

"I agree, but how do we find our purpose? I was lost for so long, attached to the idea of love and the thought that I had genuine love with Nicole. Now, I believe that I might have a greater purpose in this world. What that purpose is remains hidden to me. I'm wrestling with what that is right now," I say. Pulling a stool away from the counter, I take a seat.

Asha sloshes the yellow lentils gently in the water before setting the bowl on the far end of the counter. "We mustn't become attached but must keep searching. Attachment causes us so much pain. If we become complacent, how are we supposed to learn about ourselves and our purpose in the universe? No doubt, no awakening."

I shake my head in agreement. Asha was correct, she didn't know it, but I had allowed myself to become attached to the emotional connection I created with Nicole. It embarrassed me that I allowed myself to cling to the emotion. I was nothing more than a slave. "Isn't it all about experiences? About finding magnificence in the mundane, triumph in disaster, and the God within ourselves," I found revelation in my own words. "If I am a true seeker of self, then I can't just idly accept someone's experiences as my own. I must actively search for the thing that I want to discover. That's the only way that I see to find my purpose. I was so bogged down in the idea of a perfect life with Nicole that I lost myself along the way. A perfect life is impossible, right?"

"I believe so but isn't a 'perfect life' a paradox of sorts, or at least a contradiction of terms? How can one live a life without negatively impacting another life? For example, this bowl of lentils we'll eat tonight takes food from another. Does that other person go hungry because of it? The universe finds balance in its own way," she suggests as she places the rice cooker on the counter, fills the bowl with dry tan-colored grains of rice before adding water.

The universe finds its way, always levels the playing field. It doesn't care about me, my needs, or my deeds. Wrapping my arms around the idea that I have no control is a hard connection to make. If that is indeed the case, then is the so-called purpose I'm seeking completely irrelevant? Unchecked, the thought of my irrelevant purpose begins to feed back in my mind. Asha can sense my mind lost in thought.

She breaks the silence, "All I can say is expect nothing. You might be surprised what you discover," before changing the subject. "Shall we prepare for tonight's practice?"

"Expect nothing, huh," I repeat as I pull the plug on my feedback loop, "yes, let's do that. Maybe we can discuss this more some other time?"

"Certainly."

We move to the den. Asha summons Ziya from the doorway, "Ziya, we are about to begin. Please hurry." We unroll our mats, set our props to the side. I hear footsteps in the hall just before Ziya in her socks comes sliding in across the hardwood floors with a playful smile,

"I'm ready!"

We all chuckle as we take our places on our mats, closing our eyes, attempting to center ourselves.

With a soft voice, I begin, "Inhale. Exhale. With each inhale, a new moment begins, and with each exhale, that moment ends, and then a new moment begins again. New beginnings and endings. Birth and death. What are you going to do in that moment in between?"

Always, starting over again, again and again. Wanting, waiting, and expecting nothing.

CHAPTER 19

As a virus ravaged the world outside, I felt safe inside the constant routine of life here with Asha and Ziya. Life was simpler now that my life possessed a continual rhythm for me to connect to. No expectations for me other than to wrestle a goliath of a self into submission. Long journeys in the woods, meditating under the sheltering shadows of tall whispering pines, speaking with animals, and myself. Like a dense fog, a layer of calm had settled over me, but below that covering still boiled raw, unprocessed emotions. The universe provided me time and a place to heal, but I continued to struggle under the weight of my shackles some days.

With my morning asanas complete, I take my coffee into the backyard to meditate. It's still dark. The sun just poked its face above the tops of the trees. Something is different about the air this morning. There is an eerie quiet surrounding me. No birds chirping or insects whining. I take a seat on the wall and began to meditate. With little effort, it arrives. Nothing. I'm not sure how long I am in that *nothing,* but a sense that I am being watched brings me back with a startle. I open my eyes, expecting to find Indigo balled up at my feet, but she is nowhere to be found. I scan the darkness below the cypresses, and still, I can't find her.

Between the trees at the top of the fence perches a coyote the size of a small dog. All four paws balance on the cap of the fence post. The animal watches me with an intense glare with its wooly tail tucked tightly behind. I freeze. Now I understand why the birds were so quiet. In the whisper of a breath, it turns and dives off the fence to the other side, making no sound as she touches the Earth.

What I had just seen throws me into a mental frenzy. What was the meaning of this predator's appearance? I feel uneasy as I try to reconnect with the nothingness again. The strangeness of the interaction excited my imagination. Was there a significance to be gleaned from this encounter? I try to connect to that thought to find a higher meaning, but my nothingness rapidly becomes infested with thoughts of Nicole. I was so close but failed again.

I still struggle with the loss of my love for Nicole. Anger boils uncontrollably from deep inside me. I hate it. I felt it grow exponentially on the steady diet of the hate I fed it. My mind lost somewhere in between hate and love. It discovers a fractured sliver to the past, pulled deeper by the drag of its gravity. The agitation grows inside of me; I need to be alone. I must face this. I need to settle my mind in any way that I can. I must break free.

As the spring sun rises higher in the dome of a pristine blue sky, I think about the Victory Garden that Asha and I had discussed. Time was drifting away. Spring has snuck up on us. If we didn't get the beds dug and the plants she bought in the ground now, the chances of successfully growing anything this year would be minimal.

In the garage, I find a rusty yellow shovel and a pair of gloves. This is all I need. In the backyard, I select a patch of dirt. Bending over, I clear the small crusty white stones that litter the surface of the ground. I dig, stabbing the shovel into the hard-rocky soil. The land is so dense and compact. Certainly, nothing could survive here in this inhospitable environment, as Asha had said. There's no space large enough for life to catch hold, no room for any living thing to grow. I dig, turning the dry, dead red clay, watching its twisted clumps fall off the shovelhead. Thrust. Turn. Toss. Repeat. I become lost in the rhythm of it all. The cycle of anger and hate combined with a blind rage overtakes me. I am seething. As white-hot as the sun burning over my head. I continue to unleash my fury onto the ground.

Speaking to Nicole in my mind, "Why did you leave me when I needed you the most? Why did you hear my truth as a judgment against you? You told me you loved me. Was that a lie?" Each question creates more anger. I thrash wildly. The shovel reverberates a few dull metal thuds as it strikes the soil. "Why!?" I toss the tool down in disgust. "What is wrong with you?" I ask myself. Like a tire iron through a plate-glass window, a voice crashes through my meditation in rage.

"Can I help?" I look up to see Ziya quizzically standing in front of me.

"I'm sorry, what did you say?" shaking off the haze of the anger.

"I wanted to know if I could help you," she asks innocently with more conviction, pointing to the shovel.

"Um, sure. Do you know how to use a shovel?"

"No. Not really. Well, I've never actually worked in the yard before. It's because, well, I'm scared of bugs," she admits while shrugging her shoulders.

"Hmmm. Scared of bugs? What's there to be scared of?" I pick up the shovel, brushing dust off the handle.

"I don't know. You know, they're slimy," she sticks out her tongue while shrugging again and shaking her body.

"It's not their fault. They can't help the way they are," I say teasingly.

"I know," she answers, shrugging her shoulders again.

"If you want to help, go, grab some tools from the garage and bring them out here. You can help me dig out the new beds so we can plant some things."

"Ok," she says while walking in the direction of the garage.

"Get yourself some gloves too!" I yell.

I turn my attention back to the soil and my internal war. The battle between my ears had only just paused while I spoke with Ziya. It waited for me to reconnect to my anger and self-hate. I could never bring myself to hate Nicole. The pointy end of the knives of self-loathing always meant for me.

"Why did you have to go and screw it up? You could have been happy."

"Could I have been? For how long?"

"You'll never know because you're a coward."

Ziya returns, "Ok, here's what I found," holding an

orange-handled hand spade, corroded green garden fork with worn rust-covered teeth, and a metal rake for my inspection.

"Will these work?" she asks, unsure.

"Yes, those will work. I'm going to draw out some lines for the beds. Do you think you can dig up the soil inside those lines? It's pretty hard. The soil, that is. I'm sure you'll have no problem digging this up," I smile as I draw two large rectangles with the tip of my shovel in the Earth.

"Yeah, I think so," she replies unconvincingly.

"Here's where our first two beds will be," I say while handing her my shovel. "You can do this," I assure her.

She grabs the shovel barehanded, timidly tapping the ground with it. It doesn't make a dent. She looks at me curiously.

"Try again."

Weakly the metal shovel taps the ground, and again, nothing changes.

"What am I doing wrong?" she wonders out loud.

"You're not doing anything 'wrong.' Just try to do it with a little more power. Put your gloves on too. You don't want your hands to get all blistery and calloused." With her gloves on, she gives the hard-dusty ground a few more whacks with the shovel. Progress! The crust of the soil breaks free, revealing another layer.

"Keep going. You're doing great."

"This is really hard," she says as blobs of sweat form at her hairline.

"Yeah, it is. Go for as long as you can. When you're tired, I'll take over."

I grab the hand spade and walk to the other side of the yard, trace a line in the dirt of another bed. Drop to my knees and dig. Digging with the shovel was more manageable, but here on my knees with this little spade, I have a closer, more intimate contact with the Earth. The connection calms my mind. The anger dissipates like the tiny grains of dirt that began floating in the air.

From the shadow of the trees, Indigo appears as if to inspect what is going on in her kingdom. She walks past Ziya with all the royal grace of a queen as Ziya beams a smiles from ear to ear.

"Oh my God, she never comes out when I'm here," she exclaims with joy.

Indigo wanders towards me, finding some heavy shade under the eave of the house. On her side, with her head held high, she wags her tail, watching us toil in the dirt while she stands guard. In this calm, my internal dialogue changes. No more daggers, rage, or hatred. Unknowingly, I begin creating a message to send to Nicole:

I'm a sailor on a ship sailing a life-load of insecurities set adrift on a sea of self-doubt. Fear and its illusion of failure had left me rudderless. I was taking on water and slowly sinking. The day the tide washed me up on your shore was like setting foot on solid ground for the very first time. I was uneasy. A life alone had taken a toll on me—I was nothing more than a savage with sea legs. You took me in and gave me something I wasn't expecting—love. Your love, like the warm, nourishing rays of the sun on my skin, filled my heart.

With a whole heart of your love, I dreamed of a life together, a future. I wanted to give you everything you desired. The thought of asking you to be my wife overtook me more than once. Fear, knowing that the tide would return and take me back to sea, told me you'd say 'No, who would want a wreck of a man like you? You'll never be a worthy partner, father, or provider.' Feeling unworthy and inept, I hid from your light. In the darkness, I was lost.

In time and thoroughly unprepared, the tide returned for me. Resigned to the idea that is where I belonged, I walked back into the water. Too unaware to ask for help, I got caught in an undertow that kept pulling me under and further out into deeper waters away from us, our love, and most importantly, you.

It's cold out here. I long for a way back to your shores and the warmth of our love.

"I'm tired. I think I did pretty good, though," says a sweaty Ziya as she stands over me, holding her shovel. "Wow, you dug up a whole new bed with that tiny shovel all on your knees! I feel pathetic."

Lost in what Asha would describe as a "peeling the potatoes" type meditation, but back now. I look to see Ziya referring to the bed of dirt I'd turned. As if in some trace, I had blindly dug out a garden bed 8' x 10' and eight inches deep while composing my message.

"Yeah, well, I wasn't planning on doing that," I offer, somewhat simultaneously astonished and embarrassed. "Looks like we're ready for the next step. Are you ready to plant some vegetables?"

"Yes!"

Under the warm, healing orange rays of the spring

sun, we spend the rest of the afternoon planting squash, zucchini, eggplant, red and yellow peppers, cucumbers, rosemary, tomatoes, basil, and watermelon. Conversations about TikTok videos, the collapse of the Soviet Union, reasons why worms are scary, and the Jamestown colony are all discussed in thorough and satisfactory detail.

"Ok, all the plants are in the ground. It's time to water. Let's go to the shed and grab the hose," taking off my gloves.

Ziya walks to the shed and cautiously opens the double doors, peering from floor to ceiling to be sure it was safe. Stepping inside, she suddenly screams like God himself had tased her and runs across the yard.

"OH MY GOD! OH MY GOD!"

"What's wrong?"

"THERE'S A BUG IN THERE!" she says in a panic.

"What kind of bug?" I ask, walking to the shed.

"A DRAGONFLY!"

"Where? I don't see anything."

"Right there," pointing to the corner of the door frame.

I look up to see the hollow carcass of a long-dead dragonfly dangling in the remains of dust-covered spiderweb strands.

"That?"

"Yes!"

"Well, that's no longer a dragonfly."

"It's not its soul that I'm worried about," she replies with a snarky tone.

I laugh as I worry about my own withering soul.

CHAPTER 20

The weeks passed. Spring arrived without warning and hovered over us. Warm mornings spent in the sun meditating, drinking coffee, being petted by Indigo, and watching the garden seedlings take hold. Their delicate leaves opened and extended themselves wide to absorb all the sun had to offer. I enjoy watching the plants' progress each day. Coming inside to ask Ziya proudly, "Did you see the zucchini plants today? They are getting big!"

The consistency of life became a ritual. In that ritual, I felt whole. No longer a stranger. Journeys to the woods to wrestle my ghosts became less rigorous and more purifying. The lively chats at supper over pulses and yogurt filled me with joy. The occupants more than friends, the house more than a home. I came to lovingly refer to this home as "The Monastery"—a place for my solemn cerebration, reconciliation, amelioration, and regeneration. Undiscoverable on any map. So remote and isolated that it remains unknown to my closest friends and family, but a destination that always existed right before my eyes and pressed deep within my bones, I arrived here by pure accident but stayed out of sheer necessity.

I spent long hours here just facing it and facing myself, knowing that this path was the only way forward. It was a gift that the universe had offered me. Here, I attempted to resuscitate my belief that wisdom can only emerge if the mind is pure and calm. I finally succumbed to the hard realization that cultivating an unclouded mind can prove to be more difficult than I imagined. That true wisdom takes many different forms and can only be attained when you dare to open your eyes to witness it.

With tonight's class complete, I roll up my mat. "You both did well tonight," I say with firm sincerity. I am happy with their progress. Our regular time together has made them both physically stronger, more focused. They listened carefully to my instructions and even asked the occasional question.

Supper prepared, we move to the dining room to eat. We speak of new yogurt flavor creations. My suggestion of a flavored strawberry variety met with a unanimous "Yes!" Asha's suggestion of a honey and cayenne pepper flavor roundly discarded with tongues sticking out. We laugh at the outlandishly disgusting offerings of okra and tomato yogurt. "Yuck, I'd rather eat this table cloth." The laughter continues.

We clear the dishes from the table and bring them to the kitchen for cleaning. I fill and click on the kettle to boil water for tea before walking to the den. I pick up the old guitar with its tarnished strings and brush through a few chords while they continued to clean. My fingers fumble; my voice hums a few melodies to sporadic chord changes while smiling at the absurdity of it all. Not long ago, I was inside a double tsunami of emotional chaos surrounded by people pulling me apart. Now here I am planting gardens and discussing yogurts while the world outside slowly falls apart.

The kettle whistles irritably. In the kitchen, I pull out three teacups from the cabinet. "Who wants to tea?" I ask. I make two cups of tea and leave them on the counter. I take a cup for myself and sit down with the guitar again. More fumbling of tuneless melodies met with unintelligible verbal ramblings.

They enter the room to sit on the floor, listening with their teacups in hand as I play. I feel my face turn hot with the redness of a blush, nervous by my playing and thin voice. Feeling flush with sweat forming around my ears, I continue to strum and sing. I feel nauseous, as if I were standing flatfooted on a boat during heavy seas. The room spins and stops suddenly.

"Mr. Ian, are you alright? You don't look well," Asha asks as she sets her tea down on the floor and crouches towards me. "Your face is wet, and you look horribly pale. Perhaps you should lie down."

"I'm fine. Must be something I ate," I reply with nervous hesitation.

Asha turns to Ziya and says something that I can't quite understand. Ziya cuts her eyes to me with a serious look of concern. She hands her teacup to Asha, stands, and leaves the room in a hurry.

Asha turns back to me, "Mr. Ian, I'm begging you,

please lie down or go to your room and rest."

"I don't mean to alarm you, but I believe my throat is closing."

"Are you unwell? Do you believe that you have the virus?" Asha always jumped to this conclusion when anyone of us had the slightest sniffle.

"I don't think so," I say while cautiously taking a sip of tea and clearing my throat.

"Let's take your temperature," we move to the bathroom to find the thermometer.

I feel queasy. Legs and feet suddenly feel numb and stringy like elastic bands. My head aches unmercifully. I slump to the cold tile of the bathroom floor like a wet mop. So, this is it? This is how I die. Just when I was so very close.

Thermometer found, "Here, put this in your mouth." Asha shoves it into my mouth. The cold, blunt tip of the instrument stings as it settles below my tongue. The long, silent wait begins. With a robotic chirp, chirp, chirp, the verdict arrives.

"Oh my, 103! Let's get you to your room to lie down."

I don't understand what she said as the room spins again. Did she say 103? Impossible! I feel fine. I'm fit as a fiddle—whatever that means.

"I'm fine. It must be something I ate. It'll pass," I say unconvincingly.

I feel like a fiddle, just one dipped in wet cement. Asha pulls on my arm and yells to Ziya.

"Come quick! We need to get him to his bed."

I awake wet in sweat, the sheets soaked. I must have been asleep for days. The pain. My feet are cramped so tight that I can't feel my toes. Movement is impossible.

Every joint feels filled with coarse grains of sand. If I could only lay still, then the pain would subside, but my body won't listen. I jerk and grimace in uncontrollable fits. The pain won't quit.

"Let's recheck your temperature, shall we?" I hear Asha before seeing her in the dark, stiflingly hot room.

My glands are so sore and enlarged that I can hardly open my mouth to accept the instrument. We wait for the chirp.

CHIRP. CHIRP. CHIRP.

"Let's see here... 104. Oh, dear. Can you take some liquid? I made a tonic for you. It's fresh lemon juice, honey, sea salt, and water. Known to work wonders," she says with fake cheer.

"Ok," I choke.

My swollen tongue is fat like a shoe, and my throat is almost completely closed. Swallowing is next to impossible as most of the cool, sweet liquid runs down my face onto the sheets.

"Sorry," I croak apologetically.

"Nonsense. There's nothing to be sorry about. We need to get you feeling better. What else can I do for you? Some hot soup maybe or yogurt?"

"My feet. My feet hurt so much," I struggle to say.

"May I have a look?" Asha asks.

Speaking is too painful, so I nod my approval.

I see the horror in her eyes as she pulls back the sheets and looks at my feet. Are those tears forming in her eyes? It was much worse than I imagined. Is this the end of me?

"Well, they are quite red, puffy, and cramped. Some skin is peeling away too. Probably due to the fever," she says calmly. "Let me fetch some coconut oil and rub that on them. Hopefully, that will make them feel better. Will that be ok?"

I nod.

Minutes seem to pass like days before she returns with a small white bowl filled with oil and a towel. "I warmed some coconut oil. Let me massage your feet with it. It should relieve the cramps." Her hands began rubbing my tender, aching feet with what felt like a chainsaw. I wince in pain.

"Too much?" She asks.

I nod yes.

Thoughts of Nicole drift in my mind. She should be here with me, taking care of me. She should be rubbing my feet, but she's not. She abandoned me when I needed her. Were her words of love just a lie and vehicle to use me? Or was she too afraid to shed her own selfish needs to give herself to me? I want to forgive her, but I am too weak. The pain is unbearable. Oh, the agony is too much. I drift away. Reality, hallucinations, or dreams, it's too hard to tell the difference.

I am standing barefoot on a beach of white-hot sand, staring off into the endless line of the noonday horizon in front of me. From the corner of my eye, I see the orange arch of a fish's back break through the shallow, tranquil turquoise water. The arch breaks the plane of the water again and again. The horizon no longer holds my attention.

I have no intention of bringing her into the sun-faded yellow polyethylene net that stretches between my hands. Something in her movement tells me that she needs me. I oblige. She and many others like her willingly enter the tulle that I laid before them. Some of them are bright white with large black spots like a Miro painting, and others are royal purple with thin white stripes, all of them covered in an armor of thick scales.

Closing the net and drawing it tight, I pull the haul over my shoulder. With all the strength I can muster, every muscle fiber employed, I pull them ashore. They thrash and gasp, filling their mouths with the sticky salt air. I hurry from the sweltering sun into the shadow of the tree line. The skin of my bare hands breaking, blood flowing freely among the now orange plastic strands of netting. I must hurry through the trees and up a steep incline.

"Please be calm. I am only trying to help," I implore.

Further up the hill, I struggle, not knowing exactly where I am headed.

The hill flattens, revealing a large pond surrounded by large smooth anthracite-colored stones covered with pale green lichen. With a rush and a push, I tear the net open with a single thrust and unload my quarry into the water. Life restored!

On my knees, with exhaustion, I watch as they play happily in the deep clear water. Pride swells inside of me as they dance and flirt with each other. All except my orange friend, she is not satisfied. She arches and splashes in the water, flicking her tail back and forth to show her distaste. My smugness fades.

"Are you not happy here?"

She leaps from the pond over the pile of stones and onto the hillside below with a great charge. I'm paralyzed in awe as I watch her slide helplessly in the dirt. Tiny red ferns, twigs, and dried leaves give way until she comes to a sudden halt. Relieved, I jump into action and desperately run back down the hill towards her. I'm almost to her when I see a small child with raven-colored hair appear next to her.

She asks without emotion, "Do you need help?"

Is she talking to the fish or me?

"Yes, I suppose I do," I admit.

Bending down, taking hold of the fish by the tail with her right hand, she raises it with effortless ease off the ground. My orange beauty does not struggle or wheeze.

It amazes me.

I follow as the girl walks back up the hill.

"She doesn't want to be here," she says, nodding to the pond where the other fish continue to play.

"Where does she want to be?"

"There," pointing to a pond further towards the peak.

We continue to climb in silence and with no great rush. Arriving at another pond with its still, cold dark water, the girl slips the fish gently into the water without creating the slightest ripple.

"But she'll be alone here," I say, confused.

"Be patient." Her eyes focus on the water and the scene she knows will unfold.

The fish swims deeper and deeper to the bottom, frantically nudging rocks as if searching for something. In the water's dark depths among the stones, a form appears—her mirror image.

Finding herself, she is content.

CHAPTER 21

The afternoon sun filters through thick white wooden blinds that cast long thin horizontal lines of light across the room. A door opens on squeaky hinges followed by a frigid burst of air. I wake with a shiver as the air mixes with the moisture covering my body. I pull the bedcovers closer. I'm barely here.

"Well, how are you doing today, Mr. Ian?" Asha's voice breaks the silence.

"Hello?" I raspily ask.

"Wonderful! So you do speak. We haven't heard you mutter a word for weeks. We were beginning to believe that you didn't want to talk to us any longer," she says with a laugh.

"Huh?"

"I'm kidding, of course. You've been very, very ill."

Putting a straw in my mouth, she says, "Take some water. It will help."

I sip, choke and cough as the cold water tears at my dry, closed throat. Asha places a wet rag on my forehead as I open my eyes. I bring my hand to my eyes to wipe away a layer of salty crust to notice the skin on my fingers is fire engine red.

"What happened to my skin?" I ask with shock as I examine the length of my arm.

"Oh yes. Your fever was severe and sustained for some time. Your skin peeled and blistered because of it," she says plainly as she lightly taps my forehead with the cool cloth.

Shock rises inside me as I ask, "Are you telling me that I lost a layer of skin?"

"Yes, it appears that you did. We tried all sorts of methods to bring down your fever but were unsuccessful. Your body found its own way of protecting you I suppose. For a moment, we thought you might die."

"Die?" The loud whisper of death rings in my ears and pulls me under again.

Night sweats and constant suffocating fever, an infinite series of saccharine dreams, and acerbic nightmares pass through my mind. I'm not here. I pass through walls. I watch stars melt like cheap plastic bags, only to be reborn again. With every gentle living spirit, the universe turns black, caving in on itself, turning into a pile of cinnamon-smelling ash. Avocado green Trabants, pushing out Krispy Kreme donuts from their tailpipes, float through a sky full of chrome-colored clouds. Crimson-hued canines wrapped in barbed wire with their squared ears and menacing yellowing smiles patrol this place. Up concrete stairs, in a darkened hallway, a man wearing spectacles with extraterrestrial features waits to rubber-stamp my hand. A face covered in tattoos and pierced with millions of tiny brass rings tells me that "It's required for your re-entry, sir." The stamp on my hand reads "crutches," stings and throttles me with a raw jolt of electricity. Through a sunken doorway, a low-hung ceiling with smooth, seamless concrete walls filled with dense white smoke tickles my throat. Dozens of dirty young people with hungry eyes lounge despondently inside metal luggage carts, carrying on meaningless conversations simply to compete with the loud and constant thunder of a bass drum that shakes the entire room. There's no way out.

Suddenly and all at once, God's voice speaks to me, "The more you ignore me, the closer I get." I shake with embarrassing fear.

"An omnipotent God that quotes Morrissey?" I scoff. "'Heaven knows I'm miserable now,'" I reply with a snarky sense of disdain.

Silence.

"Ha, I bested you, God!"

"'Peace, love, harmony? Maybe in the next life!'"

"God, you are a wretchedly clever swine. You truly screwed up. You know the world would have been a better place if Jesus had been born a girl."

No reply.

I drift back to the tiny bedroom while Asha continues to talk. "Yes. The hospitals are overrun with people sick with the virus. So many people have died already. So, the fear that you might die was very real."

"How long have I been in bed?"

"About three weeks."

"Three weeks!" I am too weak to balance the gravity of what she is saying to me. I pull back the sheets to see my naked body. I almost faint as I see my loose red skin hanging over protruding bones like a deflated beach ball. Asha could see the fear in my eyes.

"You lost a lot of weight. The only food you could hold was a small amount of pulse and water rice. You wouldn't even accept yogurt," she admits as her lips close tightly.

I think about yogurt and how it might soothe my dry throat. "Do you think I can have some yogurt now?"

"Certainly, it would make me very happy to see you eat something. Let me get you a bowl," placing the wet towel on my forehead and calling to Ziya. "Ziya, splendid news Mr. Ian is awake and wants to eat yogurt."

She walks out, leaving the door ajar. Through the opening, cold air from the hall fills the room, giving my exposed body the chills. My joints ache as I pull the bedsheets up towards my face. I stare at the ceiling fan as it rhythmically spins above me like the hands of a clock. "How much time was lost here in this bed?" I think.

Seconds that I would never get back. I think about the garden we planted and wonder what had grown while I was gone. Where is Indigo? Time has stopped for me, but it kept pushing forward for everything else. There is no stopping it.

Asha returns with a glass bowl of white yogurt and a large silver spoon. "Here you go. Let's see if this makes you feel any better." She dips the spoon into the bowl, collecting a small dollop before offering it to my open mouth. I cringe a bit as the tartness of it strikes my tongue like a bolt of lightning before I swallow it down.

"Tastes good," I say as I lick my coarse, dry lips. One after another, Asha continues to offer me spoonfuls of yogurt slowly.

Ziya appears in the doorway to ask, "Mr. Ian, how are you feeling?"

I turn my head toward her, "Well, I'm alive thanks to you and your mother. So, that's a good thing, right?" She smiles as she bashfully glances at the floor. "How's the garden growing? Did anything happen while I was away? How's Indigo?" I ask.

A smile appears on her face as she replies, "Yeah, actually, a lot of things are growing. The pea and zucchini plants are getting big. I see Indigo in the mornings, but she won't come to me. I think she misses you."

"Nice. I'd like to see the garden and my furry friend soon."

"Not until you become stronger. You are very weak. You must eat to recover your strength," Asha interrupts before offering me another spoonful of yogurt.

"You're right. I need to get stronger. Ziya, do you think you can take care of the garden until I'm on my feet again?" She nods yes before shyly waving her hand with a sad expression to say goodbye and moves out of the doorway.

"Be careful of those dead dragonflies!" I joke as she walks away and down the hall. Asha smiles and offers me more yogurt, which I eagerly accept.

Nights are no longer filled with salty fits of sweat, searing fevers, or trippy hallucinations. My body is depleted. My joints continue to throb with pain when I shift in bed while my skin's redness heals, thanks to Asha's regular warm coconut oil rubdowns. I believe that the worst of the virus has passed.

From my bed, I offer my morning 'thank yous' to Buddha, who has sat resolute and unshaken during my illness. "Thank you for the lessons of peace and tolerance," I whisper out loud as I bow my head.

Asha appears in the doorway, holding a bowl of yogurt and a cup of coffee, "Good morning Mr. Ian. How are we feeling this morning?"

"Good morning. I'm feeling much better. I thought I might like to get out of bed today and go outside for a bit. I think the sun might do me some good. What do you think?"

"Ok. I believe that is a good idea. But you must remember that you are still very weak. Eat some yogurt now. I also prepared some pineapple seasoned with chaat masala. Let me get that from the kitchen," she says as she places the bowl and coffee on the nightstand beside me.

In pain, I reach for the cup, bring it to my lips, and sniff. For the first time in a long time, I sense a future—a future that is just out of my grasp, but a future nonetheless. For once, my mind is no longer dotted with visions of the past. My wrestling match with the virus left me with a new resolve. Sure, death paints a pretty picture sometimes, leaves you without a care, but I wasn't ready to give in to it just yet. Dying never phased me, but the fear of not finishing what I started in this life before I died mortified me. I raise my cup as if I am offering a toast, "Here's to life, expect nothing," and take a sip.

Asha returns with the heaping bowl of cut pineapple, which I eat with the yogurt. The chaat masala tastes strange and mutes the fruit's sweetness, but she assures me it is good for my health. Who am I to argue? She had convalesced me this far. After the bowls are empty, I ask if I can go outside. Asha agrees. She dresses me from the bed before asking for Ziya's help to get me to my feet. I wobble, sway side-to-side like a kite in the wind. They hold on tight from both sides and guide me to the back of a wooden dining room chair that Asha has brought in for this moment. I drag my feet towards the chair, grabbing a hold in desperation.

"I made it." I sigh and take a deep breath.

I gather my strength and push the chair along the hardwood floors as if it were a makeshift walker towards the den and the back door. Ziya and Asha flank me as I go forward, pausing after a few yards to take a break.

"I am so weak. It's embarrassing," I say through heavy breaths.

After about ten minutes of stopping and starting, we make it to the back door. Rays of the morning sun pour through the blinds; I desperately want to be outside and bathe in their magnificence. Ziya opens the door, and the warm, fragrant fresh air rushes over me. They both help me over the threshold to a small wooden bench that directly faces the vegetable garden. From there, I can see the elephantine-sized dark green leaves of the zucchinis with massive dark yellow flower blossoms opening their arms skywards. Behind them, on a thin line of brown twine, lounge pale green pea pods ready for the picking. Rows of cabbage clinched tight like tiny purple fists rise above the stony soil.

"I'm amazed at how fast they've all grown. Look at those tomato plants. They are huge. We'll have more tomatoes than we know what to do with."

"We will give away what we can't use. That was the purpose of our Victory Garden, wasn't it?" Asha asks.

"Yes, we'll have enough here to feed the entire neighborhood, won't we?" I say with a laugh.

I see Indigo's bright white head pop up to scan the yard from behind an umbrella of cucumber leaves. She closes her eyes and rubs her jawline on the thick, coarse leaves. I whisper to her, "Indigo, come here, girl."

"Oh, there's Mr. Ian's Zen friend Ziya," Asha says with a touch of jealousy as she points to Indigo. Ziya smiles.

Indigo hears my call but keeps her distance. She weaves underneath the woody stems in the cool dark shadows that the leaves provide as she waits for me to be alone.

"Mom, maybe we should go inside so Ian can be with her," Ziya says as she smiles with a suggestive nod to her mother.

"Yes, let's do that. Mr. Ian, will you be ok out here by yourself? Please don't move about without our help. Ok?"

"I'll be fine. I just want to be in the sun for a while and pet Indigo if she'll allow me."

They walk inside, leaving me alone in the whisper of

the morning air. I take a deep inhale of it through my nostrils, hold it, and release it across my dry, chapped lips. Again, again, and again. My breath is scant and staggered, but the more I focus on it, the more my body responds. I feel clean.

Indigo slides under the cover of the leaves, cautiously moves towards me, and jumps onto the bench beside me with a fluid leap. I continue working with my breath while she rubs her face across my bony protruding elbow. She purrs while I breathe. In that moment, we are both content.

The mist of cool spring mornings gradually burns away with each passing day. Daily visits to the garden return strength to my weak body. My skin heals, muscles grow, vigor returns, and my mind strengthens while I dance delicately with fleeting tranquility.

The flower seeds that Ziya and I planted poke their heads upwards to the sky. The tiny green peppers and tomatoes form, dangling carefully from extended branches. The bees hum, butterflies flicker their wings, while the hummingbirds float still in the air. Life is beginning to take shape again.

CHAPTER 22

I arrive at the house later than usual. The sun is almost gone from the stage of the sky. Inside, I swap my shoes for chappals. "Hello?" I yell from the garage door. No reply. I thought it was strange that no one was home. Our class usually starts at this time. I wonder where they could be. I open the back door to find them in the garden behind the young pepper plants.

"Hello," I say again from the threshold, wave with a smile.

They both turn to me with faces long and ivory white, as if drained of all life. "Mr. Ian, please come quick. It's Indigo," Asha says, waving her arms frantically for me to come.

I run and trip in my chappals before kicking them off, moving faster towards them in bare feet. "What's the matter?" My pulse increases, my eyes widen as if prepared for danger. A deluge of tears rain down their faces as their eyes connect with mine.

"It's Indigo," Ziya says, pointing to a lump of white fur behind the large dark umbrella of zucchini leaves, "I think she's dead."

In a single step, I dart towards the lump. Pulling back the prickly plants, I find Indigo's mutilated body. A large rip in her abdomen where her insides fell out into a viscous pool of blood and fluid.

"Get me a towel!" I bark.

Ziya turns and runs to the house.

I kneel beside Indigo and beggingly yell, "No! No! No!"

"Is she gone?" Asha asks with her hands covering her mouth and tears still in her eyes.

I put my face to Indigo's. There was no breath. "I believe so," I offer matter-of-factly.

Ziya returns with a pile of spotless white towels. I take one, spread it open on the ground. Using both hands to support Indigo's neck and wilted body, I place her on the outstretched towel. Her warm body falls limp in my fingers. The spirit of life has left her. Her beautiful white coat splattered with beads, drips, and crimson-colored fluid lines like the canvas of a Pollock painting. Lifeless, her crystal blue eyes shine like jewels in the last rays of the evening's expiring sun. Tucking her limbs and tail, I wrap her tightly in the towel while her lifeblood continues to ooze, soaking through the fabric.

"What happened to her?" Asha asks.

"It looks like she was attacked," I reply as I wrap her in another towel.

"Attacked by what?" a shocked Ziya cries.

"It's hard to say, but if I were going to guess, I would say it was a coyote," the adrenaline of the shock passes as the heavy gravity of sadness arrives inside me. I selfishly think about how my mornings wouldn't be complete without the soft touch and thunderous purr of this beautiful creature.

"Should we call someone? You know to remove the coyote?" the practical part of Asha kicks in.

"Remove the coyote to where? Whoever catches it, will kill it," I reply with a touch of anger. I convulse uncontrollably in pain as tears pour from my eyes over Indigo's shrouded body. After a few minutes, with sore ribs, I wipe my face with the back of my hand, "The coyote was connected to its true nature. Does it need to die, too, just for being what it was created to be? I am sad at losing Indigo, but taking another life will not bring her back. The universe finds its evenness. Unfortunately, we don't have a say in how things get reconciled. Right?" I stand with Indigo in my arms and kiss her between her eyes to whisper, "Enjoy your journey, my friend. Thank you for your lessons. I will miss you." I turn to Ziya to ask, "Would you like to help me bury her?"

"Yes," tears continue to roll down her swollen cheeks. She knows what to do as she turns with slumped shoulders and walks to the garage.

"I'm so sorry, Mr. Ian. I know she meant a lot to you," Asha offers solemnly.

I hold the bloody bundle close, rock it back and forth in a needless sway, and hum an aimless berceuse. "Yes, she taught me a lot about myself. Mostly she taught me to be patient. That to be unattached and independent, one must be vigilantly patient with eyes wide open," I stop swaying and look down at her face. "I will miss her morning purrs... they always sounded like warm OMs to me," I say with a smile littered with tears.

Ziya arrives with a shovel and gloves. The three of us walk high on the hill above the railroad tie retaining wall to find a spot overlooking the garden. I hold Indigo as Ziya digs a hole as the sun makes its gentle retreat for the day. There's nothing to say, so nothing is said. After Ziya is through, I place Indigo's body inside the deep pit; I inhale and release an OM for her one last time with my hand on her head. With the chant complete, I slowly shovel dirt over the empty vessel of her body as I cover her with the tide of Earthly time and ponder the futility of life's endeavors. We are all dust.

Ziya and I collect loose stones to pile over the grave while Asha cuts bright yellow flowers from the garden and places them on top. We stand quietly in the light of the rising moon until our tears are dry.

No asana lessons tonight; we agree without discussion. In silence, we sip on tasteless pulses, pick at bowls of cold white rice, and refuse yogurt. We clean our dishes, mumble our goodnights, and wander to our rooms to meet a sleepless night.

In my bed, I toss and turn for hours with images of Indigo in my mind. I struggle with the purpose of it all. Why did she have to die? Why in such a gruesome manner? I get out of bed, walk to the bathroom to wash my hands again and again. The blood was gone but, in my mind, it was still there. Sticky and slimy, it covers my fingernails, moves between my fingers, soaking my wrists. In a panic, I slam my hands on the marble counter and look at myself in the mirror. "What is wrong with you?

Have you learned nothing all this time?" I take a few deep breaths before dumping cold water on my face and drying it with a clean towel.

In the kitchen, I find a glass and fill it with water from the faucet. The moon shines through the window and illuminates the kitchen. I watch as the rays flicker and twirl in the reflection of the water in the glass. I turn up the glass to empty it. The house is quiet, so I make sure the empty cup makes no sound as it touches the metal sink. Sleep will not arrive for me tonight; I am positive. I leave the cold tile floors of the kitchen and walk through the den towards the back door. In the darkness, on the den floor, I see Asha sitting asleep or in deep meditation. I tiptoe past her.

"You're awake," the even tone of her voice breaks the silence.

"Yes, I couldn't sleep. I didn't mean to disturb you. I was just going outside to watch the moon," I say with my hand on the doorknob, ready to exit.

"You're not disturbing me; I'm always up at this hour. Are you going outside without your chappals?"

"Yes, I'll be fine," I reply, embarrassed that she noticed.

"Were you thinking of Indigo? Is that why you can't sleep?" she turns her body towards me. With my eyes adjusted to the darkness, I can see a large silver pot of milk sitting on a wooden trivet on the table next to Asha. She must be making yogurt, I think.

I turn to face Asha, "Yes, I was thinking about Indigo and some other things. I suppose her death and the way she died have left me with many more questions, honest realizations that I have a lot of emotions that I have not processed completely. I thought I was further along with things, but her death unraveled that a bit." I move to a seat on the floor, press my back up against the wall, close my eyes in exhaustion, and released a sigh. "Why must everything be so complicated?" I mutter without thinking. "I blew up my life because I was numb. Was I halfway through a good life, or was a good life halfway through with me?" I joke before continuing. "I chose to leap into this endless sea, to let it soak inside of me. Something pulled me here to this hostile shore of emotions to do battle for my soul. Every time I believe I have my arms around it, it slips through my fingers like water through sand. How much self-examination can one soul take?" I offer with a closed-eyed snicker. "Maybe I was better off where I was—just numb," I admit, knowing that it wasn't true.

Asha leans forward towards the pot of milk, wraps her hands around the metal sides, touching it cautiously, before removing her hands slowly to say, "As you said, 'Each moment begins and ends.' If we accept this, then we can begin to live. Everything ends, does it not? Your journey is unique. Some people seek external pleasures like money, power, or fame because it makes them feel something. In reality, they do not feel a single thing. Sometimes to be richer *is* to be poorer."

I nod in agreement as I find the truth in her words.

With the face of Tara hanging on the wall behind her, she continues, "The gold inside of our souls is of far greater value than any fortune that we might amass. Is it not? The only manner in which we can test the quality of this gold inside each of us is by fire. I know this journey you are on appears full of seemingly endless trials, painful introspection, heartaches, sleepless nights, and almost your death, but this is the inferno you must go through to assess the true value of your most precious element. Be proud knowing that you are traveling this road with your eyes wide open. Some people live their entire lives with their eyes closed or in their delusion, unable or unwilling to witness the lessons that the universe is offering them. With your eyes open, you see the pain and the pleasure is in the universe. You understand the power of your words, the nature of your actions. You are a self-aware and complete person. Rejoice in knowing that."

I pause to process her words before countering, "If I am such a complete person like you say, then why do I continue to feel so torn apart and scratched inside?"

"Have you ever considered that all your hesitations are the keys to your understanding? That the greater the doubt, the greater the awakening. No doubt, no awakening," she says with a whisper. "Trusting life is making peace with death. How can you live if you are afraid to die? So every moment begins and ends. What are you going to do with that precious time in between?"

Her words disarm and smother me like a warm blanket. Again, there is nothing left to say, so we sit in the dark silent stillness of that room, waiting and saying nothing. Waiting for the milk to cool, for the night to bleed into the day. Patiently, we wait for everything and nothing to change.

CHAPTER 23

My neck aches. Covered in a blanket, I push myself off the floor. I crack my neck to relieve the pain. No luck. Asha is gone, so too is the milk. The dark morning sunlight pushes its way through the windows.

"You're too old to sleep on floors," I groan to myself as I stand.

I make a coffee, sip on it while I stare out the kitchen window to wonder if I had dreamed of Indigo's death. A few more sips before I pour the rest down the drain. I walk into the backyard to find her grave, a mound of dirt, stones, and withering flowers. It wasn't a dream.

"Good morning," I say as I sit next to the mound of soil covering her body.

I watch the flowers and vegetables that Ziya and I planted thrive in the sun. Pettily I am envious of their successful transformations. In that instant, something inside me breaks and changes. It is time to break the cycle of time's tide. Let it all go. Part of me needs to die and to pass through, experience the monastery, Greta, Michelle, Mike, my father, Dani, and most importantly, Nicole, to find myself. Fear of the unknown kept me looking away for far too long. Now, as I stare with eyes held unflinchingly wide open inside my soul, I find love and compassion for me. It is time for the most challenging part—letting it all be.

I rise to leave Indigo to the Earth with teary eyes, whisper my 'thank yous,' and say, "Goodbye."

I walk to my tiny room and gather up Nicole's things—the tiny memories and keepsakes of our short time together. A coffee mug with a Llama painted on its side, a black swimsuit with a gold buckle, a hairbrush with a few strands of her red hair attached, a pair of vintage Ray-Bans, and a note in her handwriting that says, "You will always be loved." I scratch out a reply to her:

Thank you for loving me and showing me how to love you and myself—something that I could never do on my own. I'll see you in the next life. Maybe there, we'll get the timing right.

I fell in love with you the moment you unrolled your mat next to me.

Love forever,
Ian

I pack it all up, carefully placing each item inside a bag.

I change my clothes, skip the morning 'thank yous,' asanas, meditation, and leave through the front door. With a hurried pace, I run to the woods as a lost child runs to his mother. My mind is littered with thoughts of death, life, love, compassion, and regret as I move. The pain in my neck is a distant memory as I pick up speed with my heart pumping and lungs expanding. On the rugged dirt path of the forest, my feet feel lighter, more connected with the Earth as I run.

Needlessly I push myself up steep sludgy hills, across pools of quicksand-like mud, through thickets of vines with thorns like razors. I want my heart to give way, to explode, to test the bounds. God knows it is conditioned enough already; let this be the true test.

"Do you know God? How much can it take?"

Towards the river, along the nape of the neck of the hill, I stride with lightning swiftness. My joints primed and greased, my blood thinned, moves like oil in a hot engine. The cool morning air blows up from the river. I feel the moisture on my face; it invigorates me. I gallop along the river's edge, hearing the geese and ducks squawk in disagreement with their territorial tongues. No time for idle chatter; there is serious work to be done. Unbridled, I know no bounds as I leap over stones, sidestep fallen tree limbs, grasp at exposed roots with recklessness.

"God, if you want me? Come take me," I snort with smug confidence.

I turn up a switchback when my right foot slams flat on a root that releases a fast, exhaustive sigh like a broken dog toy. I stop, turn to see the body of a snake stretched across the trail. It is as thick as a bicycle tire with pale pinkish-tan color scales along its back. I kneel to see if it is hurt or dead. From the cover of the grass that surrounds the path appears its dark spade-shaped head.

"You're no root, are you, sir?"

He coils his muscular body, flickers his tongue as if to say, "I warned you." I back away, out of striking distance. I feel the calm rush of adrenaline arrive in my heart and know there is no danger. The tension in his body disappears as he turns his head back to the short wild grass from where he came. I watch as his dense body slowly, with a bit of swagger, moves deeper into the brush to disappear.

"So, someone *is* listening," I mutter and shrug my shoulders.

I climb and climb up through the hills, lost in a meditation of memories running silently past the clusters of white-tailed deer and wild turkeys with their red and brown feathers. I vigilantly step over unprotected roots and the occasional sunbathing lizard along a slippery trail of red-clay and moss-covered boulders. The gray squirrels and tiny black striped chipmunks don't twitch or move a muscle as if standing still out of respect—higher I ascend, where the canopy of the trees peels away like cellophane. Back among the cemetery of dead black pines, the endless Spring sky breaks through. The sun kisses my face. I turn away; I don't feel worthy. From the corner of my eye, I see the blue-crested herons, red-tailed hawks, and turkey vultures deliberately making lazy circles in the sky with their watchful eyes fixed on me.

"I need you to watch over me now more than ever," I say to them.

Onto my knees, I brush away the leaves and sticks, pull at the ground with my bare hands. The soil is soft, black, and rich with life. I dig deeper and deeper until my fingernails break and my knuckles bleed. I don't care. I'm in a trance.

"How could the vessel of my heart be so heavy and empty at the same time?" I ask myself an impossible koan.

With my chest heaving and convulsing, ready to burst, I place Nicole's things in the hole. I slowly push the dirt back, covering the contents. I beat the mound with my bloody fists as all the forest's creatures pause to watch. My heart, oh, my heart, how much more can you take? It wanted to come. So, I let it all come down.

"How long did that take?"

"Was her purpose complete?" Selfishly I thought her purpose was to give my life love and meaning.

"She was a love in my life, not the love of my life. I need to be the love of my life."

What remained of the tiny scraps of my heart knew I needed to go through her to get to me—what a horrible sacrifice to make.

"That's a stupid question."

I lay down next to the pieces of our time together and stare at the ceiling of the world. I watch the clouds gather, darken, crash into themselves with reckless abandon. After some time, I begin to melt, connect to the Earth, the universe, and myself. My mind settles as the sky tears itself open and rains down on me. Wash away my sorrows. Wash away my sadness. The world stops just for a moment to let me die and begin again.

The wind no longer screams, only carries the chorus

of the Earth's sweetest song. The river runs and runs; the sun overtakes the darkness, shines like a red-hot diamond in the mirror of the sky. After some time with a breath, life returns. I'm a dead man reborn. I rise to walk away, leaving the unfinished fragments of me behind, things I once held on to so tightly, possessions I no longer need. My soul no longer aches.

The trail narrows as it slopes upwards next to the river with its unruly, burgundy-barked rhododendrons and rotten tree trunks. Boulders, the size of houses, dot and jut out from the river's edge. Some carpeted with heavy green moss, others stripped bare from the constant pounding of the sun's rays and water's rushing. Looking south along the river, I see a large dark gray rock of compressed slate hanging over the water baking in the morning sun. It calls to me. Its invitation to stretch out and wait on its exposed face is far more interesting than anything else. I make my way there. A billow of white clouds gathers and vanishes as I strip off my clothes. My skin glows with the salubrious beams of the sun above. Here with the universe watching, I want to see what I would become.

Alone, I release a series of heavy-hearted exhales before closing my eyes. My mind grasps for something; nothingness would not do today. It wanders from random images of the snake to Indigo's blood-stained body. A few more breaths. Nature's cacophony surrounds me, the vibration of the river, the bickering geese, the wind's deafening whispers to the grass, the faint bark of an irritated dog. I connect with it all. "Om Mani Padme Hum," spills from my lips. The gift and a long-forgotten mantra buried deep inside me finds new life again.

"Om Mani Padme Hum" overtakes me without

tantalization or seductive logic. The jewel that lay hidden inside of me with all of its blemishes appears to me. I find calm as I connect with it. There is nothing else. A soul shed of ego, lust, passions, ignorance, greed, and hate is indestructible. I feel my head being pinched with an index finger and thumb, my body being pulled upward towards the sun like an ever-expanding piece of used chewing gum.

Further and further, the strands of my energy stretch with no fear of breaking. The rocks give way around me, move, and float. I pass through them as they pass through me. I see this place as it was a century before. The river narrower, the canopy of the forest denser, the air pristine, while an orchestra of a thousand extinct songbirds sing in unison. "Om Mani Padme Hum," I feel the rippling reverberations radiate in my chest, fill my throat, tumble from my mouth to join the chorus. The symphony of sound swells and never crashes as I repeat the words.

I open my eyes to find myself surrounded by strangers. An older couple sits in front of me, their faces hidden, their legs hanging over the edge of the slate, their toes dangle like bait for the fish below. Behind me stands a thin young man with a scruffy rusty red beard staring stoically into the distance. Two children wade silently in the river's heavy current. I feel connected to them all individually and as a whole. The woman in front of me with short dark hair turns, offers a smile to show me the rudraksha beads that she wears on a string around her wrist. I smile with a bow. She turns back to the river. We all watch as the river drifts to an ocean filled by a stream fed from the clouds above.

"We are all on the same journey; most of us just don't realize it," I admit to myself.

"How long will it take?"

"How much does a bag of tortoise hair weigh?"

ABOUT ATMOSPHERE PRESS

Atmosphere Press is an independent, full-service publisher for excellent books in all genres and for all audiences. Learn more about what we do at atmospherepress.com.

We encourage you to check out some of Atmosphere's latest releases, which are available at Amazon.com and via order from your local bookstore:

The Embers of Tradition, a novel by Chukwudum Okeke

Saints and Martyrs: A Novel, by Aaron Roe

When I Am Ashes, a novel by Amber Rose

Melancholy Vision: A Revolution Series Novel, by L.C. Hamilton

The Recoleta Stories, by Bryon Esmond Butler

Voodoo Hideaway, a novel by Vance Cariaga

Hart Street and Main, a novel by Tabitha Sprunger

The Weed Lady, a novel by Shea R. Embry

A Book of Life, a novel by David Ellis

It Was Called a Home, a novel by Brian Nisun

Grace, a novel by Nancy Allen

Shifted, a novel by KristaLyn A. Vetovich

Because the Sky is a Thousand Soft Hurts, stories by Elizabeth Kirschner

ABOUT THE AUTHOR

Andrew is a unique blend of yogi, IT professional, artist, singer-songwriter, master gardener, spiritual teacher, adventurer, poet, and author.

He grew up in the affluent suburbs of Atlanta and traveled the world over, curiously learning and allowing each culture to shape his personality and philosophy. Using technology to create music across an ocean, planting victory gardens, rescuing dogs, running an IT company, and guiding his flock as a yoga teacher, Andrew exemplifies the Renaissance man and is a true spiritual seeker.

He was drawn to the teachings of Zen Buddhism at an

early age by his older brother, Chris. He began practicing yoga when it was not yet widespread and found his calling as a yoga teacher soon after that. He has a strong following of ardent students who love him for building unique Hatha sequences designed to give them the template to develop their own practice. He is affectionately known as "The Machine" for his ability to push himself with a single-minded focus to achieve any goal he sets for himself. His holistic approach to life, fitness, and love resonates with all.

His debut novel 'Waiting Impatiently' is a richly textured journey of Ian, a man at the end of his tether attempting to come to terms with his broken spirit and heart through the lens of his belief system during the time of quarantine. Then, through a chance encounter, he finds himself in a place that he calls "The Monastery," where he is provided the gift of self-examination, revival, and transformation.

He currently lives and teaches in Atlanta, Georgia.

Made in the USA
Columbia, SC
29 January 2022

54976426R00124